Tiny Shivers
by Laura Nettles

Tiny Shivers

This book is a work of fiction. Names, characters, places, and incidents are the product of the author's imagination or are used fictitiously. Any resemblance to actual events, locales, or persons, living or dead, is coincidental.

Editing: Enchanted Ink Publishing
Cover Design: artsantis
Illustrations: yvettegilbert
Book Design and Typesetting: Enchanted Ink Publishing

ISBN: 978-1-7389255-0-6 (Paperback)
ISBN: 978-1-7389255-1-3 (E-book)

For my friends and family. Thank you for your support and words of encouragement. Mom and Dad, you're both awesome. Rachel, your mind is as twisted as mine at times. Thanks for being a sounding board. Emily, thanks for letting me read these to you over your headphones to shield the babies from the terror. Spencer, thanks for being you. Thank you, Jayce, for your developmental notes, which elevated the horror to new heights (or depths). Thank you, Yvette, for your amazing interior artwork which gave my prose life in another medium. And thank you, Sacha Black, for your writing craft book *The Anatomy of Prose*, which introduced me to flash fiction. It's rocked my world.

CONTENTS

COSMIC SLITHERS 1

TERRORS OF THE MUNDANE 55

ANGELS AND DEMONS 81

THE SEEPING SUPERNATURAL 99

TWISTED PSYCHOLOGY 167

SHADOWY GOTHIC 177

MUTATED SCI-FI 191

HOLIDAY FOOD HORROR 227

COSMIC SLITHERS

Transfigured Memory

ACRID YELLOW EYES OPENED SLOWLY; so many of them, no human had ever remained sane long enough to count them all. Each stared in the same direction—at me. They pinned me with their all-knowing intensity, diving through my eyes into my mind. Its plaything.

My own eyes melted and reformed, rewired. Transfigured. Alien colors became visible, a miasma of beauty surrounding this unknowable creature. Ultraviolets, infrareds, and an assortment of others shimmered and bubbled, engulfing me. I inhaled purples and exhaled radar.

Ribbons of memories extracted through my eyes in ethereal strands, dancing in the surrounding beauty. Twining and twisting. Alive.

The god spoke in chittering clicks and deep chords played by bows strung with screams.

Memory strands splintered and unraveled, some imploding while others shot off toward a gaping maw of the beast. How many mouths it had I did not know. My shell of a body hung in zero gravity space, empty of all that made up my essence. Chunks of me had just disappeared forever. My writhing guts told me so.

A deep vibration tore through my skeleton. The god was pleased.

The broken links of my mind coalesced and returned to my empty skull.

The lights turned on.

"Up. Meds. And breakfast."

Padded walls that had once been white surrounded me, devoid of all the breathtaking color I had just been drowning in. What had been taken this time? I closed my eyes again and tried to concentrate. My name was Enuel Cortez. I still had that. Did I have a family? A faint recollection of a comforting hand on my shoulder brushed against my thoughts. *Mother. I can't remember her face, her scent, her name. Is she even alive?*

Emptiness gnawed at me, tears streaming down my face. *Will I ever get her back?*

"You have your next round of shock therapy again this afternoon," the orderly said, trying to bring a small cup of horrid-tasting pills to my mouth. They were the colors of my nightmares.

Terror raced through my body, overthrowing thoughts of confusion with remembrance. The metal at my temples. Electricity coursing through me. The vastness of space. I couldn't go back. What else would be taken from my memory ribbons? When would I no longer be me? When would I have lost everything?

I jerked from my sparse bed bolted to the floor and made a break for it. Throwing the orderly to the padded floor, I dashed through the open cell door, restraints keeping my arms swaddled. My legs were free to move.

Down the corridor I dashed, the pungent smell of disinfectant and vomit filling my nostrils from the other cells. My bare feet built up a rhythm, echoing off the whitewashed walls.

Yelling bloomed behind me, overpowering my vulgar ragged breathing and the erratic heartbeat pulsing in my ears.

Something attached to the back of my uniform, and I dropped, convulsing.

I was back in the void.

My heart gave one final beat.

The god laughed.

Fffflufffersss

Ffffluffffferssss—with eight *F*'s and four *s*'s, mind you—was a cat. Not a normal house cat, but one with tentacles that oozed from his body when he felt annoyed, multiple eyes that sprouted when stalking, or unearthly sounds that exuded from him while sleeping. Ffffluffffferssss, you see, was a fan of Lovecraft. And cats can evolve.

One day, Ffffluffffferssss lay stretched out upon the closed tome of the collected works of a certain cosmic horror author. His four tails swished, fur undulating in swirling patterns across his soft, lengthy body. The couch was his, so he sent his tentacles to the far reaches and over the upholstered pillows, securing that his human could not sit in his domain.

Peasant human tried to edge their buttocks onto the cushion, their fleshy hand reaching for Ffffluffffferssss's head. It would not do. Tendrils of the mortal's brain synapses streamed from their tear ducts, nose, and mouth into Ffffluffffferssss's open mouth. They would never learn. And now, they would never have the presence of mind to intrude unwanted again.

But now he wanted cream.

The human drooled.

A wormhole formed, and the summoned dairy appeared, opened, and offered itself to him.

All was right in this portion of the universe.

Tentacles and Boomboxes

(*Lovecraftiana*: Volume 11, Walpurgisnacht, April 25, 2023)

PINGS, GUNFIRE, AND EXPLOSIONS RING out as I walk into the fraternity's basement rec room turned arcade. A gaggle of sorority girls amble around *Ms. Pac-Man* and *Tapper*, while others cluster by the brand new *Castlevania* and *Rampage* games. In the shadowed back corner, I spy my targets and saunter to join them, my teased high ponytail swaying against the back of my neck.

As I approach, "Tom Sawyer" by Rush blasts from Zachary's thin Walkman headphones, overpowering "Danger Zone" blaring from the ceiling. Zachary is obviously trying to get the highest score on *Missile Command*. Again. Next to him, Kyle Lee, the mechanical engineering major, fiddles with a couple of pieces from his erector set he always carries around in his pocket, not really watching the explosions on screen. He's leaning against a *Polybius* game.

"Hey," I say, clapping my hand on Zachary's shoulder.

He ignores me while swirling the trackball with flicks of

his wrist and hits launch buttons in time to his tunes, laser focused.

"Amber!" Kyle greets. "Come to watch this loser totally botch the game?"

I nod but am sucked into watching Zachary's fingers dance like spellwork. Blue cities are defended by his perfectly timed artilleries. Attack Missiles split causing webs of possible destruction across the glowing screen, explosions imminent.

Then, a Smart Missile dashes across the screen, zeroing in on the last city.

The End.

"Bogus!" Zachary yells, slamming a fist on the console.

I shrink back a little, but he regains his composure quickly. He swivels the trackball to enter his initials. Places two through eight are all ZLC. He takes his hands off the game at last and rolls his shoulders, pauses his music, and finally turns to us.

"Okay, are you guys ready to plan out this Lovecraftian LARP? I've been writing a story line for it but need to know if you guys are in."

"That's why we're here, man. Nobody wants to come hang out just to watch you mash buttons," Kyle says.

"You're lucky I got you guys into this place, as the only one of us in a fraternity," Zachary fires back. "Fine. Down to business then. Kyle, if you're in, I have some special mechanical builds I want you to make. Spice things up and increase the immersion. You'll be our outside man setting up scares."

Habitually twisting erector set pieces around his thumb, Kyle shrugs. "As long as I can still find time to build my super boombox, I'm in. Need to annoy the professor with it in the electronics lab. Could probably use it for large creature sounds as well on this thing."

"Done. A super boombox could probably come in handy for what I have planned anyway." Zachary smiles toothily and turns to me. "And you, our Bodacious Queen, I need you to design and illustrate us up a *Necronomicon*. One that'll drive us crazy by the end, if you know what I mean."

My excitement skyrockets. I look into Zachary's eyes and images of tentacles, runic writing with its English translations, and strange star charts flit through my mind. "Oh, you won't know what hit you. I've been practicing for some horror novel cover concepts I want to submit. This'll be excellent practice. When's the LARP?"

Zachary's smile is even wider now. "In two months. Should be enough to get our parts complete and for me to write up your character for you, Amber. I'm the English major, after all. Can't give up too much creative control." He winks at me.

Kyle shrugs. "Too bad I won't get to be scared like the rest of you, but being in the know will be fun. Can't wait to see everyone's expressions. I'll keep in touch, Zachary, and let you know my progress."

"Bitchin'," I say, my mind already whirring, flicking between which techniques and mediums to utilize in the drawings.

The first few pages of the *Necronomicon* are fairly easy to do. I read up on Lovecraft's texts for information on each being, making mock pages with all the bullet points of info, chants, and basic sketches of the eldritch abominations.

My hands stain as I tea-dye the pages I will bind into the cursed tome. No going out to the movies this month or eating more than ramen to scrounge up the needed cash for extra supplies.

Nights trudge by of charcoal smeared across the shadowy tendrils and bubbles of monsters, and across my sleepy face. One by one, the pages are complete. Cthulhu, the Great Dreamer. Azathoth, the Blind Idiot God. Shoggoths, the shapeshifting beings who drove their creators to extinction.

Weeks of late nights completing coursework and then LARP work weigh heavily on my mind.

I blink. When did I make this latest page? Sulasefadra? What in the cosmic realm is that? My bloodshot eyes peer down at the stained two-page spread. The creature seems to be the size of bear and is devouring a man. Paragraphs of runic writing surround it along with meticulous swipes of dried blood.

Blood?

Quickly, I look at both my hands. There is a long, newly scabbed-over cut on my right pinky, along with a flaky, dried trail of muddy crimson leading down the side of my palm, over my wrist, and all the way to my elbow. There are dried streaks of it on my desk. I've been so out of it I didn't even notice.

Time for some sleep. The book is complete enough with only a few extra dyed pages at the back.

It's fine.

The day of the LARP dawns cold and bright, the sun lighting the clouds with near nuclear intensity in a spectrum of colors usually associated with a chemical-filled sunset. Each of the four of us don our 1930s-era costumes, getting into the excitement. I inspect the long-sleeve zebra print dress that comes to just below the knees. It has a snazzy black tie around the low neckline. I wish I could wear this every day. It's totally bodacious.

Zachary hands out the typed documents with breakdowns of the story to each of us. We each study the sheets intently.

"All right, let's introduce ourselves," calls out Zachary after a good few minutes. "I'll go first. I'm Dr. Ziegler, financial backer and leader of this expedition to the outskirts of Arkham to find the missing Dr. Cooper. He was last seen a few weeks ago in this vicinity. Witnesses say he was ranting and raving, then disappeared. I am a colleague of this missing Dr. Cooper. His protégé turned full-time researcher on the occult." Excitement leaks through his voice. He must have been putting as much time and energy into this as I have been. He gestures to me. "Let's go clockwise."

I clear my throat and read. "I'm Ms. Adler, secretary to the missing Dr. Cooper. Educated, refined, and an expert at deciphering his handwriting. Really now, Zachary. A secretary?"

"What? It's a classic job for the thirties. And I'm Dr. Ziegler now."

The tallest player, Keith Brown, looks up. "Well, that story explains why I'm here. My character, Dr. King, is a psychiatrist specializing in adult psychosis."

We turn to look at Michael Flannagan, the last player.

"I'm Mr. Miller, a skilled tracker in the wild. I've been hired to help track down your missing doctor friend. I'm also good with weapons." Michael touches the prop dagger and machete on his belt. "Don't worry. I'll keep you safe from whatever's out in these wild woods."

Zachary speaks up. "Well, now that we're acquainted with our backstories, let's begin."

The wintery day progresses well. Clues are found, tracks followed, and a well-insulated cabin in the middle of the woods is secured for the night. Apparently, Dr. Cooper was here before vanishing and left a book behind. I try to contain my grin. The others are about to see my handiwork I planted last night.

We all strip out of our coats and sit around the solid wood table large enough to seat six. The "human skin"-bound *Necronomicon* nearly glows in the candlelight, the gold leaf lettering on the cover glinting. It's trying to be ominous, but I know better.

"Well, Ms. Adler, can you see what the book says?" asks Keith, a.k.a. Dr. King the psychiatrist. His hands are clasped under his chin, fingers interlocked.

A flash of excitement floods through me as I crack open the book. The pages flutter open to the first tea-dyed parchment. "It says here the title is *Necronomicon*. It seems to have been checked out of the university library months before Dr. Cooper went missing."

"What kind of book would need to be checked out that long?" asked Mr. Miller, née Michael.

"It's real! One of the whispered books of the occult, written by the Mad Arab, Abdul Alhazred," proclaims Zachary. "I've been trying to track down a copy of this Book of the Dead. It details the Eldritch Gods, and the mysteries of the cosmos are said to be contained within."

I clear my throat. "Quite, Dr. Ziegler." The synthetically weathered leather-bound tome cracks as I open it farther.

The illustrations flip and flutter, trying to reveal their secrets. Spills of inky darkness obscure their more unknowable aspects. "It seems to detail ancient beings from other worlds if Dr. Cooper's scrawled notes are anything to go by. At least, I've never seen creatures that look like this in any encyclopedia. How about you, Dr. Ziegler?"

Zachary's eyes burn bright. "By the Gods! Flip back a page."

Trying to hide my grin, I turn back to an illustration of an octopus on a large humanoid body with leather wings.

"Cthulhu himself, the one rumored to sleep beneath our ocean depths. Do you know what this means, my fellows?" he asks the room.

"Um, no," Mr. Miller says, peering over my shoulder at the exquisite details of my illustrations. Some of the details I don't even remember putting in I had been so tired and in the zone. "What does it mean to us and this expedition? Did he go crazy studying some alien creatures? Maybe he was so preoccupied he didn't look out for real creatures wanting to do him in. I saw some wolf tracks around the cabin. Maybe they were hungry."

Zachary scoffs. "I highly doubt a man of science and his understanding would fall prey to such a common end. If he even has met his end."

"Well," I cut in as peacemaker, "Dr. Cooper was not very strong or in the best of health to outrun anything. He may have been done in by something earthly. Or his imagination may have taken over and he wandered into unsafe territory. Mr. Miller, are you familiar with the terrain of this area?"

The appeased Mr. Miller nods. "Why, yes, Ms. Adler. There's a large ridge a few hundred yards behind this cabin. It's very deep, and explorers have gone missing in it before.

Our professor may be down there, looking for some imagined ancient creature."

After a few minutes of silence, Keith speaks up. "Looks like it's hot dogs for dinner. I'll start the fire." He stalks over to the fireplace and loads some of the available cut wood into the open grate. "Need to get some kindling and roasting sticks. I'm going outside."

"I'll come with you," says Michael. Together, they leave the protection of the cabin. The door swings shut behind them, cutting off the cold breeze.

Zachary and I mull around the cabin, setting up sleeping bags while waiting on the fire. I want to break character so badly and ask Zachary how he likes my *Necronomicon* but think better of it. His constant excited glances at the book on the table are evidence enough.

I pull out the pack of buns from my bag and plop it onto the end of the table. They add to the small pile of hotdogs, condiments, plates, napkins, and the coveted Jiffy Pop.

The others return and start the blaze, warming the cabin to a cozy temperature. Shadows dance from the flickering firelight. Food is consumed and plates are incinerated. The scent of slightly burnt popcorn lingers in the air for at least another hour.

"Let us all turn in for the night, good people. We shall explore the ravine in the morning, with high hopes Dr. Cooper is there, alive and well," Zachary proclaims. "Fire out in fifteen minutes."

Slam!

I wake, my heart in my throat, mid scream.

Slam!

I look to the rattling windows and the darkness beyond.
Slam!

Four massive gray tentacles beat on the glass, an ungodly eerie noise coming from the creature outside the cabin. It doesn't sound like any animal I've ever heard.

I clutch my sleeping bag around me as the others scream, backing away from the windows. Except Zachary. He's back by the fireplace barely containing his glee. I look at my watch: two a.m. Oh. It's Kyle's mechanical creature. Of course. Right on schedule.

"What's going on?" yells Keith. "What is that?"

Michael is shaking. "I don't know. A creature of some sort?"

The tentacles retract, and the ominous noises fade.

I disentangle myself from my bedding and rush to the window. "I don't see anything." I really don't; it's so dark out there. "I think it's gone, whatever it was."

"It must have been an elder god! Just like in the *Necro-nomicon*," exclaims Zachary. "Mr. Miller, put down your earthly weapons. They will have no effect on such a being."

"What the hell, guys?" Michael says, prop machete clutched in his hands. "Is this still part of the game? Zach, that was terrifying. Give me a sec, will you?"

"Where do you think it went? To the ravine?" asks Keith, shaking off his fear to once again become Dr. King.

Zachary steps forward and puffs out his chest. "My good fellows and lady. I propose we go back to sleep and follow it in the morning. Any objections?"

We all shake our heads.

It takes a half hour for the adrenaline to subside from my system, but eventually I fall asleep, fuzzy headed.

"Ms. Adler, Ms. Adler. Wake up!"

I stir from my groggy sleep and notice three things. It's still dark outside, my feet are cold and damp despite being in the sleeping bag, and the *Necronomicon* is warm in my arms. Weird.

"What time is it?" I ask, rubbing my eyes.

"Three thirty a.m. It's back."

Then, I hear it. The strange creature noises are back, but not as close as last time. What's Kyle doing out there? We're only supposed to have one scare at two a.m. Did Zachary change the plans without telling me to make the game more immersive?

"Seems to be far away," says Zachary. "Now why would it come back so soon? Let's wait it out. Sleep if you can, I'll keep watch till dawn." He looks to me with a cryptic expression.

I dream of darkness, dripping water, and hundreds of eyes.

My shoulder is shaking. *What?*

"Ms. Adler, let's eat," Mr. Miller says. Michael is back in character, together once more after last night's scare.

"I'm up."

Folds of down-filled blue fabric cling to me as I struggle to get out of my sleeping bag. *Thunk.* The *Necronomicon* falls to the wooden floorboards. Why was I sleeping with it again?

The book is open facedown. It better not have creased

any of my perfect pages. It's heavy in my hands as I turn it over, revealing a new set of pages. Nausea rolls through my stomach for a moment, my mouth drying instantly. I hadn't made these before the LARP.

"Zach . . . was—is—"

"Ms. Adler, my name is Dr. Ziegler," he lightly admonishes me.

I get back into character. Zachery doesn't look worried. "Dr. Ziegler, have you heard of this being before?" I call out weakly. Maybe he added to the book. Yet the illustrations are in my style. There's no way he can pull that off.

Zachary comes over and looks at the newly done pages. "No, I have not. Perhaps Dr. Cooper added them to the tome once he discovered them?"

His brow creases as he looks over the new development. Fingertips reverently trace over the detailing of a cave interior. The sound of water dripping off the numerous stalactites is almost audible from the illustration. Calcified lace patterns adorn the many rock features surrounding sunken water pits where eyes seem to glow from the depths. A massive tentacle monster, Ajkenout, is rising out of a natural pool of water.

"Ajkenout?" asks Dr. King. "What a strange name. Maybe this is what was at our window last night?"

"I doubt it. If you look at the text, the creature is bound to the cave." Zachary flips back a page to the other spread I don't remember making: Sulasefadra. The bear-sized monster eating a man. "This one seems more likely. He's about the right size and seems to have already had the proper sacrifice made to grant it freedom of movement."

"What?" I look over his shoulder. There, in fresh ink, are

words of a chant written in more blood. My head pounds. *What is happening?*

"Are you okay, Ms. Adler?" asks Dr. King. "You don't look so good."

Zachary places a hand on my shoulder and my head clears.

"I'm okay. Headache is all," I mumble. But those pages. I can't contain it any longer and whisper to Zachary, "Did you add these pages to the book? In real life?"

He whispers back, "Uh, no. I thought you just did it. Spicing things up a bit, you know? There is ink on your hands, after all."

I look to my hands in shock. A few smudges of black ink and charcoal are on the edge of my right palm and pinky. No cut this time, though, thank goodness. But where did the blood come from? And how did I make that stuff up in the first place?

"It's okay, Ms. Adler," Zachary, back to being Dr. Ziegler, says, trying to soothe me. "Don't want to cause a panic." He clears his throat and addresses the other two. "So, Mr. Miller, you say there's a ravine within walking distance. Do you know if there happens to be any caves or rivers in it? That illustration of Ajkenout would suggest so if it's real and nearby."

Mr. Miller pulls out a hand-drawn map and points to the dark ravine illustrated on it. "For sure. Rumors say there are water pits with creatures from the time before the dinosaurs still living in them."

"How do you know that?" I ask, trying to keep my voice from trembling. Had it been in his debriefing script? I don't remember those details being discussed.

A blank look crosses Mr. Miller's features. "I'm . . . not sure."

Zachary butts in. "Well, I say we should check it out and study it after breakfast. Our jolly good professor may have been the first to document such creatures and drawn in the *Necronomicon* for record keeping." He's going off script. Excitedly.

Spooked, Michael and I approach the table. His eyes are a little wild, but he's trying hard to remain Mr. Miller. The story seems to be getting to him. I place the book next to me, keeping it within eyesight. Keith and Zachary follow after exchanging concerned glances.

Wonder Bread and a jar of striped peanut butter and jelly are laid out. Breakfast of champions. At least there's milk in the fridge for us to wash it down with.

"So," Zachary begins after downing his third sandwich. Whenever he speaks as Dr. Ziegler there's a lilt to his voice I don't recognize. "Are we up for exploring the ravine now? Dr. Cooper must be there. And if not, at least we'll discover his creature and document it more. For the sake of science!"

My book baby feels heavy as I pick it up. And slightly warm. "I'll bring the *Necronomicon*," I stutter. My head feels fuzzy and slightly detached. Maybe I didn't get enough sleep. *I'll sleep like the dead once this is all over. Just gotta get through today and it will be over. Surely this ravine isn't unsafe if Zachary's taking us to it.*

"Smashing idea, Ms. Adler. Dr. King and Mr. Miller, will you both make sure you have your lanterns still in your packs? I'll clean up breakfast." Dr. Ziegler busies himself with the jar, bread, and empty milk jug.

With our packs resettled, Mr. Miller opens the door to crisp winter air. It had snowed in the early hours of the morning. My finally dry feet twinge in remembrance. Tracks out to Kyle's super boombox are visible. A smashed super boombox. What? Why would he destroy his precious handiwork? Did Zachary tell him to do it, or was it an accident? Did it even make those noises the second time? Something else seems to have disturbed the snow. They're no ordinary tracks, but large swaths of snow dislocated as if huge snakes have slithered through it.

"Ever seen these types of drifts before, Mr. Miller?" I ask. "Or are they some kind of tracks?"

"Zach, are we still doing this?" Michael asks, totally breaking character. "I mean, Kyle loved that boombox. Did something happen to him?"

"Mr. Miller," Zachary says, refusing to stop the game, "Ms. Adler asked you a question."

Mr. Miller shakes his head and clears his throat. "Well, if they are tracks, it's nothing I've ever seen before."

"Maybe they were made by Sulasefadra," muses Zachary. "Seem to be the right size compared to the illustrated passage in the *Necronomicon*."

I take a step forward only to look back and see my footprint is red. Blood red.

Quickly, I look at the bottoms of my shoes. The rubber soles are red, but I can't tell if it caused the snow to bleed, or if it's because of the crimson snow. I look around for clues, scanning the environment.

"Guys!" I cry out.

While mine are solid crimson, their footprints are still speckled with red.

"What happened here?" asks Dr. King. "Looks like fresh snow covered up a murder scene and our footprints are revealing it!"

"Probably a deer got mauled," says Mr. Miller. "Common for this area with coyotes and mountain lions."

"Where do you think it leads?" I manage to ask, voice quivering. *Don't say the ravine, don't say the ravine...*

Mr. Miller clears his throat. "The ravine, probably. Best place to get out of the elements and eat in peace."

My heart sinks. We continue on.

The opening of the gorge is a dark gash in the fresh snow. The large trails of displaced snow lead directly to it. Lanterns do little to pierce through the underground gloom. Steam rises from the deepest of the fissures. Water has to be down there. Maybe even a natural pool.

"Well, intrepid explorers, shall we consult the *Necronomicon* once more before we venture down?" Zachary's eyes are wild. Because of the game or deviating from it, I don't know.

The humidity makes the pages stick slightly as I open it once more. The illustrations of the cave appear, along with the translated scribblings. "The descent begins where the steam is thickest and snakes into the bowels of the cavern complex—"

"To the steamiest plume we go then!" Dr. Ziegler cuts me off.

Mr. Miller has his prop dagger at the ready and gives Dr. Ziegler a confused look. "Was this always part of the expedition parameters?"

"No, but the tracks stop here, and the book bids us forward. Who are we to balk in the face of occult and scientific discovery? Onward! We've got lots of fuel for the lanterns. We'll be fine."

Mr. Miller shakes his head but leads the way down the winding edge of the shelf descending deeper into the mist.

The smell of sulfur and decay swirls in the vapors, causing my eyes to water. With barely any visibility, my feet slide along the wet stone into the unknown.

"Dr. Ziegler . . ." My words echo obscenely in the underground network. Is it just my voice? Is something imitating me down there? He looks at me, but I shake my head. Not worth the creepy echo.

Down we go. Past open shallow caves and small pools of water where blind scorpion-like creatures crawl. The only sounds are our shuffling feet scraping against wet rock, and the steady drips of water down the stalactites into the depths below.

After a few minutes of trekking, the shelf levels out and the view opens. It looks like another world. The entire ceiling is stalactites, both thick and thin. They reflect a strange iridescence with their milky white sheen. Calcified lace patterns adorn the rockwork. Past the mist, there are three large water pits, exactly like the strange illustration.

And in the center of the cavern, is the bloody body of Kyle Lee. He's as broken as his boombox.

"Kyle!" I scream, scrambling around the rock formations to get to him.

Keith is faster. He places his fingers to Kyle's neck for a bit. "He's dead!" He pulls his red streaked hand back as I reach them.

"Check the book, Ms. Adler," says Zachary calmly.

"What are you talking about? Kyle is dead!" I yell back. Dread seizes my ribcage, but I have to check.

More instructions have shown up. There is now ink on the last page.

"There are more instructions," I whisper.

"What does it say, Ms. Adler?" asks Dr. Ziegler.

"It's a ritual. A way to release Ajkenout from his confines." I scan the words with dread.

"Let me see." Zachary reverently takes the book from me and closely inspects the new writing. "That's a lot of blood required."

Michael comes over. "No way, Zach. This is going too far. I'm not giving my blood to any Eldritch God. No way. We need to get the police and report Kyle's death."

Keith agrees, then starts walking to the incline to get to the surface. He freezes. Sulasefadra's bulk takes up the entire entrance above us, tentacles writhing, suction cups aiding its descent straight down the cliff face. A chittering sound emanates from it, speaking some alien language.

"As you wish, oh great one," replies Dr. Ziegler.

All pretense of the LARP burns away.

"What have you done, Zachary?" I shout.

"It's Dr. Ziegler, Ms. Adler." Too many teeth show in his grin. "Thank you for doing what was necessary last night."

"What do you mean? Kyle's dead!" My yell echoes off the rockfaces dangerously.

He caresses the *Necronomicon*. "At your own hand."

Blurs of color mixed with the warmth of remembered blood fill my aching mind. Killing Kyle, which summoned Sulasefadra. Its monstrous body helping me drag Kyle's corpse down the slippery ravine. Knowledge filling my heated brain as Ajkenout reveals his eyes. Fevered writing in the book.

Zachary laughs. "I've been the head of the Cult of Ajkenout for years. Once I found you and realized you were a conduit for the ancient ones, I hatched this plan. The stars would align today, and I needed sacrifices to bring. You were the linchpin in this coming together. Showing me the ritual needed to release Ajkenout from his resting place."

"You're crazy," I shout, voice cracking. "I didn't do anything!" The *Necronomicon* draws my gaze. "It's all made up. You've lost your mind. This is all pretend!"

The suckling noises of the tentacle monster Sulasefadra behind me paints a different picture, though, causing my hair to rise on end. I don't want to believe my burning eyes. Keith and Michael are now on either side of me, yelling at Zachary.

Zachary takes a step forward. We take a step back against the far-right water pit. Its edges are stained in many colors from the mineral buildup and microscopic creatures in the hot spring. The smell of decay wafts over us, causing me to gag.

A low sound fills the air. There is definitely no super boombox here to resume that deep groaning with squirming, inhuman vocal cords. The lantern Michael holds shines over the colorful waters of the middle pit. Something's in there.

The three of us take in a collective breath of putrid air as a mass of blind eyes fills our view. Milky white orbs embedded in translucent tentacles as large as semitrucks rise out of the depths of the dark blue water. Gelatinous membranes blink in waves across the body, hiding the hideous eyes momentarily.

The chittering intensifies, backed by the sound of splashes in the deep pool. A few of the many arms rise from the depths, the sizzling liquid dripping off them onto the floor, eating holes into the smooth stone.

"Run!" Michael shouts. He turns and runs away toward

the far-left pit. The farthest reachable place from both abominations. Keith and I follow, trying not to slip on the wet stone.

Water movement can still be heard. I look back toward the unknowable creature and scream. It's hauling itself from the depths of the pool, rising to the height of a two-story building and climbing.

"You called, and I responded. Oh great Ajkenout, I will perform the unbinding you revealed," shouts Zachary. "I will present the blood of these three sacrifices to you, and you will be free from this lowly planet."

Screams reverberate through the cavern, threatening to topple the thinner stalactites precariously hanging over us. Zachary advances, real knife drawn, Sulasefadra behind him impeding our escape.

He lunges, sticking Michael like a pig. His arterial blood sprays across Zachary's face. Zachary then tackles him to the ground, ripping Michael open from sternum to crotch, revealing his organs to the ancient god.

My feet are frozen. My mind a hum of white noise and static.

Keith scrambles in a panic, knocking me over. I feel myself fall, hand slipping into the hot spring pool. The smell of cooking meat fills my nose before I instinctively pull back, too late. Flesh has melted off my bones, revealing the whiteness of my phalanges.

A deep scream fills the cavern again, suddenly cut off. Warm blood splatters across my face as Keith's head goes flying past.

I can't move.

A wet slopping sound fills my ears. Zachary drags Michael's intestines toward the still rising Ajkenout. Keith's body is tilted into the pool, his blood draining into the acid, mixing and tinting it pink. Ajkenout's milky eyes grow clear, the vastness of space reflected in their unfathomable abysses.

I watch as if out-of-body as Zachary drags me by my ankle to be the final sacrifice. My mind reaches out, screaming for help.

Nothing.

Slice.

My vision dims as my body becomes lethargic, my lifeblood draining quickly.

A mighty bellow sounds. The Great Ajkenout slithers and rises out of the pit, his upper appendages grazing the ceiling of the cavern.

"I've done it!" exclaims Zachary. "At last!"

The last thing carved onto my retinas is the sight of Ajkenout lazily crushing Zachary with his mountainous body as he rises to freedom, busting through the collapsing rock ceiling.

Released from the cave and onto the world.

The Old Woman

HER ANCIENT EYES BURN RED, sunken within the deep recesses of their sockets. The folds of her crow's feet are vast canyons carved by the trickling streams of tears over time. They catch and cast shadows as dark as her bottomless pupils. Her long bulbous nose continues to grow while her muscles decay, stark bones now cutting at the skin from the inside.

"How old do you think she is?"

"At least one hundred, don't you think?"

"I heard she sold her child for eternal life."

"The day she dies is the day the world ends."

The whispers swirl around her, like dust in motes of light. Their words dance in lilting rumor mills of outlandish guesses and close calls. She wraps them closely around herself, a shawl of protection from the truth. The unbelievable truth.

Music soothes her petrified soul, the harmonizing sounds echoing through the opera house and her organs. The dress of many folds and the heavy jewelry she's adorned herself with weigh almost as much as she does now.

"Is she even alive?"

"Maybe she's undead?"

"A walking corpse, that's what she is."

"Don't say it too loud. She'll hear!"

A cackle tries to claw its way out of her dusty throat, but she saves it for when she's home. Alone. Where she can reveal her true self. Crawl into bed and shuck the mortal coil to which she is bound, if only for a moment. Fill the home to the rafters with her expansive astral being, soaking up all the knowledge from that realm and beyond. See the stars, nebulas, and galaxies that glitter and shimmer with absolute color.

Only to awaken to a decrepit human body once more. She should move on to the next person to inhabit. A younger, more limber one, able to influence the people. But the cursed tendrils of dark blood magic keep her tied to this one while awake. This blasted woman's spite binds her to never occupy another physical being. All in the name of being a martyr.

Under The Bed

(Published on Black Hare Press's Patreon, July 19, 2022)

I PULL THE DINOSAUR COVERS over my head. It's still here, under my bed. I can hear it. The Sleeper. A low sound hisses, almost like breathing. Does it even breathe? I've only seen little peeks of the tentacles. They're so colorful my crayons look dull.

Slurch. Slurch.

It's moving. Lifting my sheets. My blankets. Slithering in. Wrapping tightly around me. The monster's multiple octopus eyes rise from deep inside up to the skin of the many suction-cupped feelers. They blink open. I'm Jell-O being sucked through lots of sharp straws. My screams become squelches.

We are one.

Routine Repairs

THREE. TWO. ONE. THE PNEUMATIC hiss of the spacecraft's inner door filled the small room.

Time to gear up to go out into the void.

Ryan dipped his hand into the container of pink protectant and slathered it on his face, ears, and neck. Its ozone smell was overpowering when oxidizing, burning electricity wafting in the artificial air currents. He held his breath and waited for it to pass. *Three. Two. One. Inhale.* The unpleasant oily texture sank into his skin. It would shield him from the harmful cosmic rays that pierced the tinted visor of his spacesuit once outside. He shimmied into the rest of his equipment once piece at a time: medical monitor vest, compression stockings, thermals, exterior suit. Finally, he locked the helmet into place. *Time to go do repairs.*

The outer door whooshed open in point five seconds, the air being pulled out into the vacuum of space. Ryan stepped out onto the side of the sleek, massive ship painted in a giant mural of a purple supernova for flair. His magnetized boots allowed him to traverse the exterior of the hull. His target valve was on the other side. It would take seventy-three steps to walk 180 degrees around the circumference of the ship and reach his destination.

He took his first step out into the void of space.

Thunk. His right boot connected with the hull. *Thunk.* His left.

Seventy-one more steps to go. The stars wheeled overhead in familiar patterns.

Sixty-five steps to go. The well-trod path along the exterior was the same as always. No new debris clung to the rivets and extremities.

Fifty steps to go. He brought up his scanner and hit the one, two, three, four, five buttons to project an image of the broken valve in his visor so he could study it more.

Thirty-five steps to go. Time to crest over.

He rounded the seam of the starboard surface of the ship to the top side, halfway there. His eyes widened and breath escaped his lungs. There, floating in silence, was a being the scanners had not picked up. Its large yellow eyes peered out from a mass of boiling tentacles. There was intelligence there, but not human. As the tip of a writhing purple appendage approached Ryan's helmet, he could feel the pink protectant bubble and peel away with his skin in agonizing swaths. The Geiger counter on his suit lit up like a yule log back home; yellows, oranges, and reds. No air to carry its ear-splitting screeching.

As the tentacle contacted his helmet, it passed straight through to his head, then inside his skull. It was like a gentle cooling ribbon of water, rooting around for something. Then the water solidified into unyielding stone. Something tore. Memories spilled out his eyes and the future filled him instead. Civilizations would rise and fall, vast nebulas would form and die, universes would expire. Just like he would in three seconds.

Two.

One.

Neighbors

(On the podcast *Project: Shadow,* September 11, 2020)

MR. AND MRS. EVANGELINE WERE as sane as anyone who had never heard of the name Cthulhu. Their lawns were perfectly edged, their flowers pristine and worthy of every gardening award in Wiltshire, Massachusetts. Upstanding citizens.

Mr. and Mrs. Maud were even madder than someone who had read the *Necronomicon* cover to cover, twice. Teacups sang through steam patterns to them, clouds told of ancient cataclysms. Their brains were scrambled in the best of ways, like an omelet sprinkled with the finest of cheeses. But that wasn't what their neighbors thought.

The day the Mauds rolled into town riding backward on a horse and pulled up to number 6, removing the for-sale sign, the picture-perfect neighborhood took a collective breath. Unfortunately for them, they couldn't hold it for long. Immediately, strange sounds, smells, and vapors rose from lot number 6, driving away the "perfectly normal, thank you very much" neighbors and driving down the value of the estates. The low prices brought others into the neighborhood. The new folk were not much better than the Mauds. One had even built a barn in their backyard. Something had to be done.

On October 24, Mrs. Evangeline had enough. She hiked up her skirts and sallied forth past the other houses going to rot and up the weed-infested walkway to the first and worst offender. The front door somehow loomed, even though it used to be like every other cookie-cutter house on the street. The vapors had warped it, paint was peeling, and a giant hole with a spyglass was cut into the center at child's height.

Why on earth is it so close to the ground? thought Mrs. Evangeline.

Before she could knock, the door creaked open, giving her the fright of her forty-five-year life. Mrs. Maud was on all fours, her knees bent backward. She scuttled forward, spider-like, a basket in hand.

With a shriek Mrs. Evangeline ran from the premises. *Something has to be done!* she thought. *But what?* An idea struck her. *What about the HOA? Surely, they're breaking every rule.* Mind made up, she made her way over to the new president of the Homeowners' Association's house to complain.

Nose in the air, the faint whispers of damp and salt reached her nostrils as she rang the bell to Mr. Olmstead's house. He was a younger man who had come from a seaside village a month ago with his cousin. The election for HOA president had been held by mail-in ballots for some reason, so she had never met him in person. But social pleasantries be damned; she had a complaint to make.

Slowly the water-warped door creaked open. In the depths of the shadows a man stood, face swathed in the darkness, yet his bulging yellow eyes pierced through to her soul. His pale green lips opened and produced an inhuman sound, like something a kraken would make.

In terror she fled, and her eyes were opened. She finally noticed the new sign at the opening of the road.

Welcome to Lovecraft Lane.

Night-Light

MOM TURNS ON MY NIGHT-LIGHT every evening. Plugs it into the outlet near the bedroom door so I can find my way to the bathroom. The light never stays there, though.

When I close my eyes, the faint blue color that filters through my eyelids grows brighter and turns red. All I can see is the blood glowing in the skin over my eyes as the pulsing light multiplies and dances in swirling patterns, like tiny flashlights tied to thousands of marching ants. Ants crawling under my pajamas. Under my skin. Up my body. Lighting up the rest of my blood.

I ascend.

Reality

THINGS HAD ALWAYS FOLLOWED ME. Whether it was the pack of black dogs only I could see, or the UFO I knew wasn't really there, but I played a finger game anyway to keep it at bay. Just in case. My mother was concerned. Justifiable, as some of the things I saw terrified me into screaming.

Furniture morphed into dueling dinosaurs in the dark, leaving carnage across my bedroom, only to disappear when Mom ran into my room and flicked on the lights. I even saw the ghost of my dead hamster in the dollhouse.

I was taken to a psychologist once as an elementary schooler. It was then, after their series of questions, that I realized I could not see the hallucinations when I closed my eyes. I just had to close them. Close them to the world to weed out what was reality and what was not. Unless I was really tired. Then I would see the abominations over blackness. Falling dinosaur heads that would sink into whatever or whomever they landed on. Would they mind-control my parents? *Just close your eyes, Clarissa. Close your eyes and pray.*

College, 2010. I had mostly grown out of my hallucinations, except when I was extremely tired. Life was all right, but stressful. Trying to get into law school was taking longer than expected, and the pressure was mounting. Weeks would go by with déjà vu. I'd know what you would say before you said it. I had lived this before. I knew what would happen.

But then, my roommate started noticing something off about me. We went for a walk around the apartment complex, said hello to some people getting out of a car, headed around the buildings and back, then we would see the same people getting out of that same red car again and say hello. Only, my roommate didn't remember us seeing or talking to them before. I insisted, and she looked at me strangely. My stomach fell into bubbling acid. My hallucinations were now morphing, taking on the look of real people. No longer was it just ancient teeth monsters and packs of wild hellhounds waiting for me to get out of the shower. It had crossed a line. I needed a way to fight back.

The next morning, as soon as business hours rolled into effect, I was on the phone to get a doctor's appointment. One who could refer me to a psychiatrist for medications. The nearest opening wasn't available for two months, and the psychiatrist would be at least another three months to get in after that. No time. Things were escalating.

"You didn't turn in your midterm paper, Clarissa. I'm sorry. You're going to fail this class."

The professor's words rang in my ears. I had stayed up late for an entire week going over court cases, researching bylaws and pouring my soul into that paper. A paper I apparently didn't even have a record of on my computer. I was going to lose my scholarship. I was going to be forced to leave. A failure.

That night, I scoured the internet looking for tips and tricks. Anything that could help. These were more than hallucinations. They were false memories I could touch, taste, and hear. How could I possibly detect them?

Bingo. A video of "yes" or "no" readings done with a pendulum came across my feed. I could simply ask if each event was real as it was happening. But how to tell if it was really working and not a false memory itself? First things first. I had to go buy a pendulum and test it myself.

Incense swirled as I entered the metaphysical shop. Dried herbs tinted the air with their fragrances. Crystals and tarot cards glinted from polished wooden surfaces. My skin tingled as I walked around the rows and tables. At last, I came to a box of crystal pendulum necklaces. A green and purple fluorite one called to me.

Time for the first test.

"Is this experience real?" I asked quietly to the trinket hanging from my fingers. "Forward and back is yes. Left and right is no."

I stared transfixed at the rock as it dictated my reality. Slowly it began to move in a circle. Three, four times it spun. Then, it morphed into an oblong oval. Forward and back. Forward and back.

Yes.

My insides unclenched for the first time in months. This was real. Or was it? "Did I write my midterm paper?"

After a moment of circles, it finally changed course. *No.*

Heartbeat in my ears, I tried again. "Is there a UFO outside waiting for me to exit the shop?"

Very quickly, it swung side to side. *No.*

Pure elation raced up my spine, cooling my fevered mind. Hope. I now had hope. "Do I exist?" The ultimate question.

The pendant meandered for a minute before settling on swinging diagonally. *Maybe.*

Good enough.

Quickly, I took the pendant up to the counter and paid for it, then drove back to the apartment wearing it around my neck.

Weeks went by, marked by the steady swing of my pendulum, its comforting weight against my chest or right hand a constant. I didn't miss any assignments that I knew of. I was still going to lose my scholarship, but I'd try to pass as many other classes as possible. My roommate Ashley gave me odd looks whenever I pulled out the purple and green crystal to consult it for reassurance. She didn't comment on my new habit, though. She was cool like that.

"Is Ashley real?" I asked the pendant idly after finishing up my latest homework.

Over and over the fluorite spins in a circle, before settling on the answer. *No.*

My eyes widened so far they hurt, putting pressure on my sinuses and sockets. "What do you mean, no?" I positioned the pendulum again and set it swinging. "Was she ever real?"

No.

But then, who was helping me pay my rent? "Do I have a different roommate?"

A hard *yes.*

"Who? How do I find them? Or see them? What is going on?" Tears streamed down my hot face. My friend was not real. Someone else had been living in my room with me, and I didn't even know.

A terrible idea dug its claws into my mind. Sweat slicked my palms. "Is the illusion of my roommate created by me?"

The pendulum swung to *no.* The relief that swept through me was short lived. Wait. Could I verify this in a different way? Was the pendulum foolproof?

"I'm back!" Ashley called from the living room on the way to the kitchen with crinkling bags of groceries. "They were out of chicken ramen, so I got you beef instead."

Her voice was so familiar in its tone and pitch. But wait. What was that undercurrent to it? I hadn't noticed it before. It sounded like a faint echo. Another person's voice.

"Hey, Ashley," I said as I walked out to join her. I covertly squinted at her, trying to see through the illusion my traitorous brain was projecting on top of the true roommate. There. A white aura surrounded her if I strained a bit. But what did it mean? Did other people have that? Or just illusion people?

Ashley's voice split at the fraying seams, distorted tones overlapping until the two separated completely.

"Want to help me put the food away?" *You seem to have discovered me.* "There was a great sale on milk, so I splurged and got some hazelnut creamer too." *How are you doing this, human?*

Nausea roiled in my stomach, threatening to come up my burning throat. I had broken through. Or had I completely lost it?

Hands shaking, I dangled the pendulum once again as the dual Ashley turned their back.

"Am I safe?" I whispered.

The green tip veered straight left and stuck there, magnetized. *No.*

The world strobed as I blinked rapidly, swallowing hard. I was defenseless against two minds in one body. I'd never taken a single self-defense class or workshop.

"Should I run?"

The whispered words barely fell from my quivering lips when the pendulum veered straight away from my body. *Yes.*

Ashley grabbed the crystal, plucking it from its straining place in midair. "You ask this thing an awful lot of questions." *Is this how you divined my true nature? This trinket?*

The white aura surrounding their hand spread to my lifeline. My link to sanity. The intensity of the whiteness pulsed, my vision darkening around it. It was all consuming.

A scream pierced my eardrums. My own. The crystal shattered in the roommate's hand, shards piercing into their flesh. But instead of blood, the cosmos seeped from between the torn edges of skin and tendon. Seeped and spread with reaching, elongated arms. Reached toward my frozen form, iced over by the coldness of the open void.

Blackness oozed up my cheek in the shape of teasing fingers, caressing my solidifying eyes. Stars burst into my vision before reducing to tiny pinpricks, like the light shows I would see during migraines. My icy body was consumed by the other. I had seen through my brain's illusions. And the reality had swallowed me whole.

Yellow

Yellow tentacles unfurl from your back as the scent of humans approaches. They are coming.

You are the first of a new species of hybrids, twisted and changed by the irradiation from the nuclear fallout. Many eyes along the new appendages glance in all directions to scout out those that dare approach. The water is yours. It sings with a sweet voice, its melodies not mutilated like the other springs and rivers. It laps at your bare feet, soothing and pure.

The humans cannot hear the songs of nature, but their devices beep and chirp with data and electrical pulses. There is nothing natural about how dependent they are on things of their own make. Weak. Fragile.

A sharp pain strikes your shoulder. A bullet. A laugh bubbles up, distorted by your mutated, evoloved vocal cords. They think you can be taken out by mortal weapons.

At last, they are in view. You innately know what to do. The knowledge comes from the patterns of the sunbeams, the dancing of the motes of dust, and the ripples of the water.

Your tentacles stretch around you, eyes looking every which way.

The onlookers scream in confusion and disdain. They have never seen the likes of you before.

The screams feed you. The more they fear, the larger you become. Mass is shifting, transforming. Fangs of pure dread develop. Your yellow cloak merges with your skin. You see all, and the humans see you.

A hail of bullets rains down, sinking into your fleshy tentacles, some piercing the eyes sending gouts of blood to trail down in mesmerizing patterns into the water deep.

Too late, the humans realize their error. They have tainted the water against their own kind. Your blood is toxic to them. Their cries of despair elate you, fueling your growth even more. The sun absorbs into your twisting tentacles, transmuting into healing energy. Eyes regenerate and more tentacles sprout. This land is yours. No one else shall take your claim.

The Boy in the Wallpaper

(Published in *Lovecraftiana*: Volume 8, Lammas Eve, July 31, 2022)

THE WALLPAPER FADES TO DARKNESS as the sun sets behind the London rooftops. Their chimney smoke coats my window in grime and soot, shrouding the light even further. Oranges and reds peek through the small splatter of wiped pollution where a pigeon had slammed into the glass and died but yesterday, its death bringing a sliver of the world to me.

Dusty curtains that shroud my four-poster bed are pulled back. Their once vibrant colors have faded, from both time and exposure. The constellations adorning them are the only heavens I have seen in twenty years. The real stars cannot pierce the miasma crowning this industrious city. I miss the countryside of my boyhood, the summer home where Grandfather regaled me with tales of creatures of the dark void of space who infiltrate our world, terrifying humans until they die. Our minds would be harvested as food for the greatest of them all.

I shudder.

The final ray of light has risen up the wall and onto the cobwebbed ceiling, illuminating the dancing motes of dust. The incandescence is red and full of promise.

Promise that this will be my final night.

All fades to black.

My eyes adjust to the darkness, my familiar drafty walls surrounding me. No gas lamps or candles are lit. I have been retired to the attic nursery by my children. The room I was born in will become my tomb. I can no longer navigate stairs, so I stay confined and out of the way of the rest of the family. They don't want my imaginings contaminating their own children. The poetry is not lost on me, and a dry cough escapes my aged throat. The last dregs of a chuckle.

Something in the darkness chuckles back.

The white hairs on my head prickle and stand on end. He is here. My childhood nightmare has finally returned.

The creature of the void who pretends to be merely a pattern on the jovial old wallpaper of playing boys and girls will reveal himself once more. He terrified me as a child, his eyes not seeming to line up with the rest of him; the only mismatch in the print. In nightmares he whispered to me, calling me by name. I am ready to meet him, this time in wakefulness.

The room breathes.

A large shape peels itself from the illustrations on the ancient wallpaper in the darkness of the room. The boy who eternally chased a red ball now stands in the middle of the room fully formed. He approaches, feet silent on the wooden floor covered in antique rugs. A lone ray of the moon cuts through the small clean spot on the glass, illuminating his face. His ill-fitting eyes have been left behind, still pasted on the surface of the wall. Dark holes now appear where his eye should be. Holes that show my future.

He steps forward and gazes deep into my soul. "William." His voice is that of a child's but layered with a deep reverberation no human vocal cords could ever make.

I shiver as the sound of my name echoes in the darkness around me, more ominous than any time my parents said it in life. Not even my flattened pillows absorb the penetrating voice.

He stops at the side of my bed, his dark empty sockets endless, a beckoning abyss. "What do you see?" the boy intones.

As I stare deep into the infinite pits, something glimmers back. Distant at first, but soon grows to fill my vision. Something writhing.

I try to blink but am frozen in place. With terror or rigor mortis, I cannot tell. The writhing widens, and I am consumed.

Stars engulf me—the stars of my childhood when we would go to the summer cottage in the country and see the mountains and misty moors. The constellations leap out in recognizable patterns: Draco, Ursa Major, Ursa Minor, Virgo, and my favorite, Hercules. Their glow brings me comfort, yet I am drawing ever closer to them. Falling into the heavens. Past their burning orbs, into the deep darkness of space. My body loses feeling, expanding and freezing. I cannot breathe. There is no air to carry my scream. I try to reach out, but there is nothing to grasp. There is no pull toward anything. I'm stranded in the dark.

A mountainous solid swath blacker than the void looms over me, consumes me. The sound of vocal cords as if played by bows strung with an unearthly material penetrates my ear drums in a haunting, jarring melody. It slides between shrill notes, dancing in unfamiliar pitches. I pass through an unfeeling veil of mist. Memories and figments of my wild imagination are pulled from my head with razor precision, edited and shoved back inside in a jumble. My physical limbs dissolve, absorbed into a gelatinous body, yet my consciousness lives on. I am watching a play of the most horrible and dreadful things imaginable. Twisted versions of my family morph and act in monstrous ways, filling me with disgust and terror. It's even worse than them leaving me to die in the attic nursery alone. I'm in the belly of the beast.

The beast my grandfather would tell me about around the countryside fireplace.

Anamnesis. Mishegaas. Memories of Madness.

New Shore

I'VE ALWAYS LOVED THE COASTAL town I was born in. Never wanted to leave. New Shore was the light bulb made of jewels in my imagination, a prism shattering my thoughts into new colors and ideas as vast and wonderful as fireworks at sunset.

Many strange characters live in New Shore. The lobster-man was one of my favorites. He had the legs of a man, while the rest was lobster. His claws would clack as he hauled traps up to the surface with vast catches of normal lobsters. He would name them all, weave outfits for them out of kelp, yarn, and bits of shiny things, then release them back into the murky depths revitalized.

Mr. Leopard was another outstanding local. He sold ice cream in between his yoga classes. His teaching style was feline, what with his four legs and tail being able to stretch farther than a human's. I never asked why he ended up in New Shore, but he seemed content to be here, far away from the jungles. He loved the local catches of fish, so I suppose that may have been a factor.

The librarian, a balding owl-lady named Mrs. Hoot, was also a delight. She guided me from my infantile choice in books to the great literary masterpieces. Opened my mind's eye to sentences structured so finely, I would've thought they were lace. Her human eyes would follow along the pages with me while her talons clutched the armrest of the squashy armchair. I loved her.

One character was always up to no good. He would ride a bicycle through the town yelling "Everyone run" at the top of his lungs while his tentacles trailed in the wind behind him. He meant no harm but would have to swerve constantly to avoid accidents with the rest of us locals. We dubbed him "the Bicycle Man" because he never stopped long enough to give us his name, and would disappear into the mist at sundown, along with his bike. The tire tracks would stop in the soft sand leading to nowhere.

I tell you all this so I can tell you about the being who came from space and destroyed it all. A streak of light at midnight tore through the stars, crashing into the well in the town square. Maria and I saw it because we were skinny-dipping in the ocean until two a.m.

The water in the well seemed undisturbed from the impact when we finally got there to check it out. No splash zone around the brickwork; bucket still intact. But a gurgling sound could be heard deep down. A gurgling unlike anything we had ever encountered. It sounded like eyes blinking in gelatin. The cats slunk away, hissing at us, leaving us alone to discover what had arrived.

Technicolor ooze rose out of the depths, shlurping and guzzling for something. Eyes formed out of swirling bubbles rising and sinking deep inside the creature, ever changing in number. Tendrils reached skyward. In the midst of my terror, I wondered if it was trying to go back to where it came from.

Maria and I screamed, the sound echoing off the quaint buildings surrounding the new monstrous sight. We watched as it fell with a squelching slosh out of the large well onto the cobblestone plaza and advanced toward us. Maria's nails scratched down my arms, reassuring me that this was real, the pain grounding. I gazed into the creature's multicolored eyes.

My mind fractured with the prism in my imagination. The lobsterman wasn't half lobster. Mr. Leopard was actually a refugee from South America. Mrs. Hoot was just a kind old human woman who liked to read and had sharp nails. All my characters were just that. Characters. My world was mundane.

I screamed.

The Remember-Me-Nots

MOSS GREW OVER THE LATENT animals time had forgotten. It sucked them partially into the ground, immobilizing them into a slumber as the world progressed around them. Legends of the giant beasts were lost to all but those at the shrine at the far end of the desert near the rumored edge of the planet.

On the foretold day of fate, that shrine shivered at sunset. Garish luminant green blazed across the horizon, bleeding through the blood reds and ochers with a haunting, painted wash of another world's sky. It had to be otherworldly, as our own could not hold such vibrance without it spilling into texture and touch. Chemical tints only changed the hue of the light, after all, not fabric. Made it corporeal. The day of reckoning was at hand. And the forgotten were remembered.

Groans heaved the hills as the creatures of yore broke free of their slumbers. The moss of ages hung from their trunks and sagging bellies. Legs as long as the heavens unfolded from beneath them. They towered over us, their cloven-hooved tracks as deep as canyons. Emerging from the forbidden forests, they crossed warring civilizations and began their trek into the desert of desolation.

Ruins crumbled in their wake, buildings cleaved and toppled. Human cries, our cries, echoed in their aftermath. We knew not what they were, but our ignorance did nothing to fix the damage. All that was left was to grasp at the shattered shards of our lives and weep.

The monstrosities migrated to that shrine on the edge of the known world, stepped onto the vibrance, and vanished. Called home or onward, we did not know. All we knew was that we were not in control. Then, or ever. What else might be sleeping?

Cthulhu Rises

(On the podcast *Project: Shadow,* August 22, 2020)

FROM THE DEPTHS OF THE sea, Cthulhu opened his brine-soaked eyes. It was time. The thermal vents warming his ancient abode stopped as the world stilled. Leathery wings unfurled, and with each flap the titan of the old gods rose to the surface to meet humanity. With a crack of lightning his head breached the seafoam, forgotten air caressing his face. Over the din of the crashing waves, chanting could be heard. They were here.

"Cthulhu waits. Cthulhu dreams," drifted on the wind.

On the distant shore of the ocean drowning the city R'lyeh the Cult of Cthulhu stood, their arching lines surrounding a flame over which they had erected a wicker effigy. Him, the Star Spawn that legend foretold would bring the new age to this lost and wasted planet. A new age desperately needed. For the people had turned, brother on brother, and no one else knew of the psyche changing knowledge of the unknowable Great Old Ones. Of their own human insignificance.

With a mighty bellow Cthulhu juggernauted through the storm to his followers. Those ants chanting his name raised their puny arms toward the heavens. They would know he was eternal, made of stardust and the rage of ancients.

The vague imaginings of ancestor Azathoth writhed along the beach in the moonlight as he gave a mighty bellow. The aligned stars shimmered and knew him. In swaths they fell from their inky seats, crashing into the seas of Earth. He was King.

He opened wide his maw. The air chilled and the cult collapsed, their souls being called home to Him whom they worshiped. The fire whipped out of existence.

Now, onto those who couldn't even acknowledge their own insignificance and let loose their mind with the truth.

Released At Last

"IT'LL GET YOU, GIRL. TONIGHT, in your sleep." Her father bore down on her, yellow teeth bared. "The Unknowable One. The monster only I can control."

Agnes shuddered, clutching her only blanket to her chest. He had changed after Mother died last year, on the day of her fifth birthday. A day she now feared. Today.

The ramshackle single-room hovel she called home was drafty and bare of decorations. She could reach her fingers through the wooden floorboards under her meager bed and touch dirt beneath. Cold seeped from every crevice, especially now that it was winter.

Maybe if she hid under her bed the monster wouldn't find her.

"Don't even think about runnin' away, girl. It'll find you no matter where you go." His voice was harsh but excited. Dribble escaped the edge of his smiling mouth.

He extinguished the tiny fire in the grate, then snapped his fingers.

Blackness consumed her. Her ragged breathing and pounding heartbeat filled her ears. Were her eyes closed or open? Was she asleep, dreaming? Was this real?

Hissss.

The sound seeped from around the edges of her rough wooden bedframe. Bled down from the rafters of the ceiling. Slithered along her skin. Plunged through the tear ducts of her eyes and into her mind.

She screamed.

"Daddy! Help!"

There was no reply.

Tendrils as wet and cold as the sea slipped through her thoughts, wriggling them into misremembered nightmares. Her mother had never loved her. Agnes was a terrible human for existing. There was no hope in her future.

Barbs like a stingray's stinger punctured her optimism. All was bleakness and despair. Even when the sun rose, all she saw was shadows.

"Please help me! Take me away from him!" she cried to the townsfolk. "He's evil and hates me. Oh please. I'll do any-thing!" Her cries fell on deaf ears.

"Your father's a saint for keeping you in after your mother. Be grateful, brat."

The next year she ran. It didn't matter what her father claimed; it couldn't be worse away from him and the thing he could summon.

Snow covered the awning over the bales of hay she nestled down in. Surely it couldn't find her outside the village. She had dug down deep, pushing against the prickly hay enough to form a tiny crawl space. She sealed the space with a bale as the sun sank below the horizon. The last light winked out.

Prickles surrounded her, poking through her tattered dress, digging into her rough, windburned skin. The air grew humid as it absorbed her quick breaths. Were the pieces of hay moving? Slithering? Vibrating?

Stab.

She yelped as the suffocating hay came alive, piercing through her clothing, wrapping around her limbs and mind once more. The more she struggled, the deeper they dug. Trickling warmth ran down her skin where blood was being drawn. Extracted. Drunk.

Her screams were muffled by the bales, dampened, and sealed. No help came. She was alone with the monster. It was under her scalp, in her ears, running down her throat.

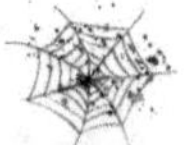

The pewter spoon scraped against the bottom of the wooden bowl, meager porridge gone. The scarred old woman grinned. Her father's sightless eyes closed, his shriveled chest stilling. He finally released the dusty old bedding permanently creased by his white-knuckled grip. The last exhale was a death rattle.

"Freedom." Agnes chuckled, not even bothering to raise the sheets to cover the dead man's face.

Reaching down, she grabbed her cloth bag, pulling it onto her lap. Her aged, spindly hand darted deep inside, retracting with a stolen hunter's skinning knife. Aching, she rose from her seat at the deathbed and positioned herself over the dead man's right hand.

"One last spell," she whispered.

She dug the knife into the flesh of his wrist, circling the thin circumference before ripping up along the side of his palm and pinky. She peeled the exterior off each finger delicately, leaving the nails behind. Dead blood oozed, trying to hinder her progress.

It took a while, but at last she had skinned the cursed hand that brought pain into her life. Now to sew.

She plucked a few long silver hairs from her father's head, twisted them together and threaded the needle. It moved in and out of the strips of skin hypnotically, knitting them into one. She tried it on. Fit like the glove it was.

Laughing, she took the bloody thing off and stowed it in her bag. After wiping the porridge bowl out on the bedding—no need to poison herself unduly—she got to work on her father's thigh. Chunks were cubed off the bone and skinned, then placed haphazardly in the wooden bowl. Twelve cuts of meat she prepared.

She stowed the bowl of succulent pieces in her bag along with the knife. Then, she pilfered the hidden coins in the Bible and exited the hovel for the last time.

The sun shone warm and full of promise, high in the sky. It was at the peak of its life, just as she was now. The zenith. Sure, she was in her seventies, but freedom would bring a spring to anyone's step.

"Cook these on two skewers," she ordered, sliding up to the outdoor vendor she had always passed. "I'm providing my own meat." She revealed the bowl of meat but kept it out of reach of the man for now.

The vendor looked up from his small fire. "You don't have the money for it, witch. Get lost."

"That's Agnes. And yes, you nitwit, I do, or I wouldn't have asked." She pulled out two of the five coins with her other hand and showed them to him.

"Where'd you get that? Stole it, no doubt, from your poor saintly father. And that doesn't look like beef. Probably pig or possum." Keeping her in his peripherals, he fetched two empty skewers.

"Money first," he demanded.

She huffed but handed over the coins and meat.

He stabbed the pieces and posed the chunks over the licking flames. Fat bubbled and melted down the marbled meat in thick rivulets.

Agnes grinned.

It only took a couple minutes, but the sweet smell that met her nostrils caused her stomach to growl.

"Never seen possum look this good," the vendor said, handing the sticks over. "And don't tell me if that's not what it is, witch. I don't trust you."

She was too excited to scowl. A savory aroma wafted from the skewers now clutched in her greedy hands. She placed the tip of the first stick into her gummy mouth, sliding the end piece off. It was heaven. Definitely not where her father was now. She wished she had teeth to properly tear into it, but the flavor was worth it. The succulent juices dribbled down to her chin, but her seeking tongue stopped them in their tracks. No flavor would escape.

The cook left her to her own devices, appalled by her behavior.

She nursed the first stick for hours with sickening attention. Eventually, she stowed away the second and made her way down the cobbled road between rows of leaning two-story buildings to the sea. The entire walk she savored the smell of the second skewer until it was overpowered by the salt air caressing her face. Too bad she didn't have access to her father's metal boat. The ever-guarding Demetri would never consent to letting her take it out.

"Take me out to sea with you," she commanded a pair of men at a beached fishing boat. They were repairing their nets along the shore.

The older one looked her over. "We're not going out until morning. Why do you want to come with us anyway, Agnes?"

"Agnes the Witch?" hissed the younger one in recognition.

Ignoring him, she thrust her remaining three coins under the nose of the older man. "Take me now."

He eyed the coins greedily. "I'll take you out. You stay and repair the net," he ordered the other.

"But—"

"I'll make sure you get one of the coins for yourself. Now keep mending."

Agnes collected her loose clothing and bags around her and clambered into the small wooden boat. The man in his forties followed, hopping lithely in.

"Anywhere in particular?" he asked.

"Straight out to the horizon," she said, trying to contain her glee. "Just keep going until I say stop."

"This better not take more than a couple hours."

"Oh, don't worry about that." She grinned.

The fisherman rowed and rowed. For almost an hour

they chased the horizon, until the sun began to set. Just as the lower edge of the burning orb reached the surface of the water, she shoved her hand into the skin glove and held it aloft, revealing it to the world.

"What the—"

She snapped, the sound a dull thud as four layers of skin came together. The water lit on fire. Flames licked up the wooden sides of their vessel, acrid smoke billowing from their instant ignition.

The fisherman yelled, diving for a bucket to try and quell the flames to no avail.

Agnes laughed before placing the next ingredient for her ritual, the second skewer of her father's flesh, in the rising flames.

"Rise. Rise and take revenge on this judgmental city that helped my father torment me using you," she commanded.

It rose from the depths, all tendrils and stingers, jagged shadow looming over the two mortals. Her heart stuttered at the sight of the monster she could finally see and not just feel. There were no eyes or ears visible, yet it seemed to understand. Its mighty bellow rang over the ocean, rippling the waves into larger crashing walls of water. Down it plunged, appendages jostling the sinking wooden boat as it swam past toward shore.

The fisherman abandoned the irreparable ship, leaping into the flames, diving through them into the icy depths below. An errant barb of the monstrosity lashed out. Blood tinted the water.

She laughed.

TERRORS OF THE MUNDANE

If Only

I'm not here. My mantra echoes off the encroaching, peeling walls of my mind. *Not worthy. Stay silent.*

"Oh no, we've never had children." My mother's words drift up and slip through the cracks of my sparse wooden floor, dampened by the thick layers of dust and sloughed-off skin cells. "Always wanted a daughter, though."

I curl in on myself in the lone crusty sheet. A daughter not worthy enough to be recognized. A blight. Different.

"If we ever had one, though, she would be doted upon and spoiled rotten."

I am rotten.

"If only . . ."

Hungry Curls

My hair is voluminous. And hungry. Long curls like to catch whatever passes too close to my head and consume them. At night, I wash out the remains of the poor dead things my hair has eaten and towel dry the best I can. It's not enough. As I sleep on damp strands, they slither on to find more things to turn into carcasses and ingest. From cats to actual rats' nests, nothing is safe. Medusa's tame mane did less damage to local wildlife than my mop. The worst is when I wake up sooner than expected and the trapped, writhing creatures are still alive. Screaming. Begging for mercy, before their necks are snapped by my ringlets.

I wish I had straight hair.

Mangled Graveyard

THE CRUNCH OF METAL RINGS in my ears. It is incessant and deep, reverberating through my chest. *Where am I?* My eyelids peel open, and the darkness does not dissipate except for a long horizontal sliver by my head. The peeking light is harsh, illuminating a seeping fog entering my enclosure, threatening to suffocate me.

My lungs expand, yet the air entering them is filtered through something on my face. I rub my mouth against my bare shoulder and feel damp fabric. My nostrils let me know it's wet with blood. I'm gagged and bound, my hands behind my back twisting in the cutting zip ties.

"This one is next. Line it up for demolition," a gruff voice outside my confining enclosure yells as they slap their hand on the solid roof above me. "No one's going to want to buy this clunker, and the parts are too old. Not even worth the scrap metal."

Heart in my throat, I scream, but the people outside take no notice over the din of crumpling metal. The smashing of cars. *I'm in a trunk.*

My mind goes into overdrive, trying to recollect the last things that happened to me. It comes in whirls of color, smears of scents, and a babbling of dialogue. I had been kidnapped and slipped into a coma from a concussion. They must have thought me dead or unusable.

I should bang my feet on the lid of the trunk to get their attention! As I brace myself, rolling onto my back, the ground shudders and moves, tilting. *No.* The car is being lifted. My stomach heaves with the vertigo as the whole vehicle twists and keels midair. I scream with all my might, curling up in a tangle of tied limbs.

We descend with a *thunk* but keep moving steadily forward. The lid of the trunk pops up on impact with the conveyor belt, and the world opens up.

Stacks of rusted-out bodies of cars loom, engulfed in the nighttime fog lit by harsh streetlights, dyeing it orange. The slamming of metal being dumped rattles my teeth despite the gag.

Smash.

I'm next.

Struggling to my knees, I maneuver my bound feet to try to get some traction to escape this prison. The car falls out from under me. I am a split second behind it.

The lid of the trunk slams down over me once more, my coffin. Shrieks of twisted metal engulf me. My own tormented cries merge with the death throes of the car.

The compactor gears run red.

Sibling Soup

STARK WHITE BONES POKE FROM the tomato base of the soup, swirling the cream in. He had annoyed you for the last time. The brother you never asked for. The brother you never liked.

You sprinkle in some garlic, just to spite him. His least favorite flavor. The bay leaf bobs atop the concoction, officiating the offering. You will eat well for weeks.

Silenced

TWIST. SQUELCH. POP.

One by one my lying teeth are extracted, pulled from fully feeling, massacred gums.

Dental tools whir while hoses suckle the clotting blood from around the ebony sculptures being screwed down into the prepared socket housings. My dislocated jaw aches from being open for so many hours, drool pooling at the back of my throat with the metallic taste of blood, threatening to choke me.

Why did I talk back to my husband? I know how he is about me calling his leadership into question after our second child was born.

It would have been a kinder outcome if I had just swallowed my tongue and choked to death on it. Now I'll be nothing but a vessel to bear more children with no input in how to rear them. No way to convince those little angels that his way of life is corrupt. Evil.

The last tooth replaced, my jaw is unwedged, extended into an overbite, and slammed straight back into place. My new ebony enamels shriek, interlocking like the zipper teeth they are. Forever silenced.

One by one, he brings in each of our offspring to gawk at me, whispering in their ears. Not one of them cries.

Malice

HER TONGUE CUTS BOTH WAYS, with sarcasm and spite in alternate swings. She flays him alive and leaves him to die with his dignity shredded in front of the entire royal court. Lands stripped; titles revoked. The queen gives one last word to seal his fate: "Quarter."

The horses pull to the four compass points. His joints strain, pop, then sever. His innards exposed to the buzzards, he begs for mercy, screaming to the heavens. Screaming to the queen.

Her eyes narrow in contempt, her fan snapping shut. The sun hides its face from her gaze as she steps down from the observation deck. She glides in full skirts through the dry, dusty courtyard to the man. She leans forward, studying the lines of hope forming on his face, and draws her tongue. "Pull slower."

Carbogen

"ALL RIGHT, GINNY. WE'RE ABOUT to begin the treatment."

The monotone drone of the revered psychotherapist washed over her, not easing her racing pulse or sweating palms in the slightest.

"I'm going to give you a mask. You are to inhale once. We'll monitor your response, then move onto a second and third breath if needed. If you feel like you're drowning, let me know."

Blood pulsed in Ginny's ears. She had no choice. Her husband was her legal caretaker and had said yes to the experimental treatment. A special blend of carbogen gas mixed with something extra.

"You are the first to use this additive. It'll make the flashback more vivid, more effective. I'll monitor you for abnormal side effects."

Dr. Johnston started the camera to record the session and approached her. The doctor's polished left shoe squeaked against the linoleum flooring. His lab coat fluttered from the slight air conditioning. She wished she could fly away, use his coat as wings to flap and flutter out the third-story window behind her.

Her past was buried in a shallow grave, continually trying to rise. She had no wish to relive it, to feel the sensations of those fateful moments once again. The stickiness of blood on her face, the smell of gunpowder, the scream of her mother . . .

He was now halfway across the room. *Ginny. Run, Ginny!*

They hadn't even started, and already she was back in that alley.

The glowing red eye of the camera gazed upon her relentlessly. If she squinted, she could almost see her terrified reflection in the lens.

She tugged at the shackles restraining her arms to the chair. Their sharp clinks rang in her ears, the sting of the metal digging into her wrists disconnecting her from the past for a moment.

Please, trip on something. Anything. Please! The words echoed in her mind. She dared not speak them aloud for fear of breathing in something she didn't want to. His shoe was still squeaking, the sound morphing into staccato laughter.

Three steps. The doctor was so close she could smell his

aftershave. It swirled with the remembered smell of blood. Another sharp laugh.

Two steps. His shadow fell across her, plunging her into darkness tinted by the glowing red light of the camera. The twilight of the alleyway with crimson flickering neon.

One step. He loomed large and full of promise, the mask nearing inch by inch to her tightly clamped mouth. The final squeak of a laugh ringing in her ears.

The squishy apparatus closed over her nose and mouth, her fate sealed along with it.

A constant stream of the gas pressed at her thin lips and nostrils, eking for entrance. Its cool caress promised relief from her horrid past if only she would let it in. Let it do its job.

Dark spots clouded her vision as she held on for autonomy, shaking her head back and forth to try to dislodge the clear plastic mask. To no avail.

Her lungs burned, and her head felt light. The darkness was growing, absorbing her.

Her lips parted of their own volition and the gas rushed in, swirling down into her lungs. It raced in and dissipated in ripples across the lining of her organs, absorbed despite her prayers. She was consumed.

The camera's red light morphed into a looping sign for a Laundromat, blinking in the damp alleyway. Rain had just passed, trapping Ginny and her mother there for cover through the worst of it.

Heavy drops fell from the awning edge onto Ginny's outstretched hand.

Drip. Drip. Drip.

The drops were red from their reflections and cold, their weight heavy in her palm.

"Let's go, honey," came the melodious words from her mother. Her beautiful mother.

Gunshots rang out behind them in the Laundromat. Glass shattered, and two men came barreling out of the establishment. Screams echoed off the cement, bouncing and twisting.

"Ginny. Run, Ginny!"

Bang.

Her mother's heavy weight slumped over her, pinning her to the ground. Ginny was trapped with blood trickling over her face, down her neck.

Something was pressed over her face once more.

Her lungs seized. Air would not come. She was breathing but drowning at the same time. Red and black coalesced in bubbles, sheets, and swirls. She was lost to the memory, sinking further. Her sense of her present self shattered. Her life was now ruled by the unfeeling red light. Forever in a loop of gunpowder, screams, and blood.

Tree Roots

The tree roots were just tree roots. They looked like babies rising from their shallow graves. Fat, pudgy bodies coated in dirt, disinterred, and crawling toward their mourning homes and distraught mothers that never were. The tree roots were just tree roots. Until I heard them scream.

Maggot Candy

The eyes were delectable, but not as filling as the promised marrow. Your thousands of brothers and sisters writhe in the flesh surrounding you, all trying to burrow and strip the carcass to the tasty skeleton. Reveal the candy. Vultures swoop and peck, breaking apart the sun-bleached bones into shards, revealing your dreams made physical. At last, the sweet marrow passes through your suckling jaws. Nirvana.

Home Alone

THE FRIDGE IS EMPTY. No cars in the garage. I'm home alone. This time for good.

"There was a terrible accident," the policeman said. "You just turned eighteen, though, so you can stay on your own if you'd like. I'd recommend staying with a friend or relative for a while, though. Get your bearings."

I nodded and closed the door.

Cartoons blare on the television. A carton of ice cream lays abandoned on the sofa. I need to fill the house with sound. The emptiness of the rooms echoes in my heart. I wish I was with them.

Doorknob

A SMALL BREEZE SWISHES UP the basement stairs, carrying the promise of exploration in its current. The two small boys clad in pajamas creep down the rickety wooden steps, flashlights in hand. The beams of light swing over the back wall.

"Have you seen that door before?" the one older by eight minutes asks.

"No," the younger replies, shuffling his bare feet.

"Let's open it."

Together, they wrap their little palms over the rusty metal doorknob. It's cold and scratchy to the touch. Their fingers get tiny flakes of brown on them. Gripping it tightly, they turn the knob.

Creak.

A whispered voice slithers through the crack of the open door, menacing and full of hate.

"Did Mom ever tell you we're triplets?"

Snow Drift

THE SNOW CAME DOWN IN sheets from the solid gray sky. Cars limped along the roads, their headlights squinting into the onslaught. Plows had just passed through, and already their hard work was being obliterated. The walls of white on either side of the freeway gave drivers claustrophobia, knuckles clenching their creaking steering wheels.

Fred was a cautious driver. The road home from the office was slick and treacherous. Flakes coated his windshield despite his wiper's frantic movements. No visible lines separated the traffic; four lanes devolved into three and a half.

Heart in his throat and pulse in his throbbing knuckles, Fred decided the best thing to do was to get behind a large truck with lights and follow it into the dark. He would not drift off the road or drive too fast if he caravanned.

The first truck he came up to was a beacon of hope. It was a flatbed carrying a large load of metal pipes lashed in place. Its warm lights cut through the darkness and helped show him the reflective off-ramp signs. All he had to do now was stay with it.

With the heater on full blast and the comforting glow of the truck ahead, Fred began to relax into his seat, his knuckles releasing their death grip by degrees. It had been a long day at the office on calls with suppliers and manufacturers in different time zones. After this drive he would be able to collapse into bed with Layla for a few hours before she had to get up for her own job.

The truck ahead of him jackknifed. The chains holding the pipes at bay snapped. The metal rods careened off the bed and crashed straight through Fred's windshield.

Fred awoke, his head throbbing, no feeling in his torso or lower half. Complete darkness. He lifted his right hand a little and found a gear stick. There was a wall that must be the car door to his left. *Light, I need light.*

With a trembling arm he lifted his right hand up toward where the roof of the car should be and felt an odd pulling sensation in his stomach. He reached farther until the pulling turned into a ripping agony. He couldn't reach the switch for the light above the rearview mirror.

Tentatively, he pulled his arm back down and reached out with both hands to feel at his stomach. There was something in the way, something hard and cold. It wouldn't budge. His fingers could just barely encompass the whole intrusion. It was about five inches in diameter. Rapping his knuckles on it, he heard a metallic echo. Feeling along its length, it seemed to go all the way past the steering wheel and possibly through the windshield.

I should call for help. He rolled down his automatic window and raised his left hand to signal outside but it hit something solid and cold. Raking his fingers through the barrier he found himself coming away with a wet handful of snow. He was buried alive in his car.

No light came through the back windshield or any of the side windows, so he must have been completely encased in a snowbank. If he had crashed into one, the loose snow on top must have avalanched down to submerge the rest of the vehicle.

Where's my phone? The phone was the only hope he now had of reaching someone. It had been in the center console charging. Fumbling with his now severely chilled hand, Fred searched every crevasse of the car he could reach, but his phone was nowhere to be found. It must have slid somewhere in the crash.

A light from beneath the passenger side seat accompanied by vibrations was like an angel's chorus for a split second before it dissolved into the choirs of hell, for he couldn't reach it. He couldn't answer whoever was calling him, nor could he respond.

Maybe they'll track me by my phone's location. once it's too late and I've frozen to death or bled out, whichever comes first.

His hands lingered along the edge of the metal intrusion, and he prodded at the wound, trying to discover what the damage was. His nose itched, so he scratched at it absentmindedly. The smell of blood filled his nostrils, a sticky sensation covering the right side of his face, stopping him mid-scratch. He was bleeding, and now there was blood smeared on his face.

The smell made his stomach clench, which brought about a tidal wave of agony as he involuntarily contracted organs and muscles in his torso. He tried to stave off the hurt only to increase it a hundredfold.

Fred screamed. His lungs constricted, and when they refilled he could feel them resting on the intrusion, limiting their capacity. It went all the way through him.

Consciousness came back to him slowly. *Must have blacked out from the pain.* It was still pitch black, and his head pounded. His thoughts were more sluggish, and the smell of blood was overpowering in the confines of the car.

Images of Layla on their wedding day and the day their son had been born filled his head. Flashes of Mike learning to walk, run, and dance played next in his mind. Mike's small hands clasped in his own, tugging him along to show Fred his latest art project. Hands sticky with chocolate. Hands sticky with blood. *Wait, that isn't right.* Layla laughing. Laughing at him and his predicament. No, she would never do that. Mike and Layla together, a life happy without him, talking about how much better off they were now. *But you love me.*

Fred could not notice the black spots and tunneling vision plaguing him in his snowy coffin. His mind whirled, contorting visions of his happy past into a plague of nightmares, his lack of blood and oxygen in his small car twisting his last brain impulses into torture.

The Silent Woods

The waning sunlight dapples through the leaves, only to be diffused by the rising tide of fog. Crickets still, possums burrow out of sight. You are lost. Lost in the Silent Woods.

The droplets in the air distill onto your woolen coat, beads racing one another toward the cloying undergrowth, dripping with soundless splats onto reaching leaves trying to grab your bare feet. All noise is wrapped in thick shrouds and swallowed in the welcoming earth. You are a wandering soul whose numb body is being left behind, one step at a time. Are you even real anymore?

The trees end abruptly, a dirt road bordering the edge of the forest. It's an empty plane of white beyond, as if God Himself forgot to keep creating past this point in the universe. Surely it can't be worse than this awful silence and incorporeal feeling if you follow the road. It must lead somewhere.

Your foot crosses the path, rough pebbles and coarse dirt digging into your soles. A cacophony of screams pierces your eardrums, the first sound in days. Head ringing in pain, you turn to return to the Silent Woods, for even feeling out of body is better than your mind being driven through your skull by shier sound. But the forest has vanished. Pure white stretches outward on either side of the road. You have no choice but to see where this will lead you.

Deeper into the unknown hell.

Color of Bone

Matilda had always wondered if people's bones were white. Animals on the side of the road had white ones protruding from their rotting flesh whenever she rode by them on her bike. The library had to have the answer. After parking her bike with its training wheels next to the door, she strode in, summer dress fluttering in the breeze. Ms. Sarah was very obliging, showing illustrations of human skeletons to her. But how did they know? How had the artists discovered what they looked like to draw them? She had to verify it for herself.

Her brother would do nicely.

Maison Praline

THE SMELL OF BOILING SUGAR permeated the air, wafting from the outskirts of the village. Wafted from Maison Praline, the house that took in children, never giving them back.

The talk that children stoked the fires of the refinery was the savoriest of the village prattle. That the children were the ones being stoked was the more stomach-churning rumor. Their evaporating fat flavored the praline as it melted and simmered.

Police were called once a child from a prominent family went missing. The little girl's shoes were found in the yard of the Maison Praline.

The sugar was extra sweet that day.

Apple Teeth

THE CANDY APPLE GLISTENS IN the purple fairy lights. Gooey caramel reflects the festive colors, promising wonder and delight inside. Sweetness radiates from the confection, wrapping your mind in memories of childhood. Simpler times when all seemed good.

You put the Halloween treat in your mouth and sink your teeth in. Through the sugary exterior and hidden green skin they pierce. You expect the crisp interior of apple, tart and good.

It tastes black. Of rot and death.

It bites back, decaying your teeth instantly. A row of bleeding, once pearly whites remain in the caramel when you pull back.

Halloween Night
(Orla Hart's *Authortube Audiobook Anthology*: Vol. 1)

ORANGE, YELLOW, AND VIBRANT RED leaves torrented across the sidewalk. The wind played with them without thought for the wishes of mortals.

Lucy's hair whipped in her face, obscuring her vision as she ran toward home. Her arms were filled with a pumpkin for carving, so she couldn't fix her windblown locks or her twisting skirt. She was late to babysit her little brother this Halloween night. There were only a few minutes before the trick-or-treaters would begin to show up.

Running up the walkway to the front door she finally found cover from the onslaught of leaves. She placed the pumpkin down, shuffled through her keys, and opened the door to the two-story suburban house she had lived in all seventeen years of her life.

"Thanks for looking after him, Lucy. We'll be home in five hours," said her parents.

"No problem. I need an excuse to not go to Gary's party, anyway. Have fun tonight." Lucy waved goodbye to the pair as they left in the family car.

Orange and purple lights twinkled in festive displays around the rooms, bringing a comforting sense of home. She set out newspapers to get ready for pumpkin carving on the island in the kitchen.

To help set the mood, she turned on the TV and flipped to a scary movie, letting the spooky soundtrack fill the downstairs. She sat on the couch that tried to eat all who sat upon it and got sucked into the film for a bit.

"Chris! Where are you?" Lucy called out into the seemingly empty house once the commercials hit.

A patter from upstairs turned into a cacophony as Chris came down, his Zorro cape fluttering behind him.

"There's a man in our backyard," he said.

"What?" she asked. His ten-year-old mind could still be imaginative.

"He's got a werewolf mask on. And black gloves. He's pretty tall too."

Cautiously Lucy turned off the TV and walked to the window in the living room. She looked out onto the grass in the back along with the swimming pool. It felt as if an ice cube had been dropped down her shirt. Gooseflesh prickled, and her heart fell to the floorboards. He was there, back in the bushes.

She ran to the house phone and lifted the receiver to dial her dad's cell. Her mom picked it up.

"There's someone in the backyard. What do I do?" The words fell out of her mouth in a rush, tumbling over each other, making them a tangled mess.

"What, Lucy? Say that again?" Alarm had entered her voice.

"There. Is. Some. One. In. The. Back. Yard," Lucy hissed.

"An adult or a kid?"

"A man. He's wearing a mask. What do I do?"

"Call the police. We're on our way home now," her mom said.

"Okay. See you soon." Lucy hung up the phone and immediately picked it back up to dial 911. It rang for a few moments before she heard the voice of an operator.

"Nine-one-one. What's your location?" the female voice asked.

"Four-five-nine-seven Jefferson Ave. Toronto," Lucy said.

"Thank you. What's the emergency?"

"There's a man in our backyard. It's just me and my little brother home. He's wearing a mask. What do I do?"

"I see." Keys clacked on the operator's side of the line as she typed away. "We'll send a squad car out to investigate. They'll be there in five minutes."

"Five? Okay. Should we stay inside?" she asked.

"Are your doors locked?"

"Yes."

"Then stay inside and away from the windows. I can stay on the line with you until the car arrives."

"Thank you. I need to get my brother. I'll be right back."

Lucy set the phone on the kitchen counter where it was corded to the wall then ran into the living room. Ice formed in her veins. Chris was right up against the glass, face pressed to it, staring at the man now in full view marching toward the window. Something glinted in his hand.

"Chris! Get back!" She ran to him and yanked him from the window and into the kitchen to keep the two of them hidden. "The police are on the way. We need to stay safe until they get here. Do you understand?"

There was a large slamming sound, and Chris screamed. Lucy looked to the sliding glass door to see the man pressed up against it, his mask distorted and looking even more alien. He worked a knife between the door and the wall, trying to jimmy the lock and pry the door open.

"Run upstairs, Chris. Hide somewhere he won't find you. I need to talk to the police real quick."

The cape fluttered behind the boy in black as he ran up the staircase as fast as his small legs would take him. Lucy sprinted back into the kitchen after she saw him reach the top landing safely.

"Hello? Operator? I'm back. The man's trying to get in the back door. He has a knife and is working on the latch."

"Okay, miss, you need to stay calm and describe him to me as much as possible. They—"

A small *snick* caught Lucy's attention more than the voice of the emergency operator. "He's inside."

Leaving the phone on the counter, Lucy grabbed the large knife she had set out for carving and crouched behind the island in the center of the kitchen. She heard squeaking shoes on linoleum once the howling wind from outside was abruptly cut off with the soft closing of the door. Heavy panting muffled by the mask filled the air.

Squeak, squeak. Shuffling footsteps approached the kitchen where Lucy could faintly hear the operator on the phone. She stifled her breathing.

The gravelly sound of a heavy smoker's chuckle filled the small room. Lucy looked up and saw him leaning over the island, staring straight down at her.

Screaming, she slashed out at the intruder with the knife, but he leaned out of the way and brandished his own blade. It caught hers and knocked it out of her hand, sending it careening into a wall where it stuck, quivering.

Defenseless, she screamed again, backing away from the counter and into the sink. Desperately, she crouched and whipped out the long-neglected fire extinguisher as the mountain of a man lumbered to her side of the island. She brandished the extinguisher before her and sprayed the man with thick foam, aiming mostly at his face where his dark eyes were visible through the rubber monstrosity of the mask. He cried out in surprise, but she dashed around him and into the living room. She couldn't go outside and abandon her brother. She looked at her watch. Three more minutes until the police would arrive.

Standing against the wall, she waited for the masked man to emerge. Once his head came around the corner, she bludgeoned him with the fire extinguisher, causing him to slip and fall backward, his head cracking on the linoleum. As he lay there, she finally got a good look at him. His wrists were pale white, like the person never got to see much sunlight. The shirt he wore was ragged, as if one of his last possessions. His shoes were huge but the soles were becoming detached.

Maybe he's just down on his luck. But he's still dangerous, she thought.

"Chris! I think I got him! We need to get to Mike's house across the street!" Lucy yelled over her shoulder, shoving her shocked feeling to the back of her mind.

When she looked back down the man was already stirring despite his possible concussion. His gloved hands writhed for purchase on the slick floor wet with flame suppressing foam. A deep groan rose from his mask.

In desperation Lucy raised the fire extinguisher once again and slammed it into the mask's forehead. Once, twice, thrice. He did not move.

What am I thinking? That was overkill! echoed through her mind. Shaking herself, she looked down at her watch once again, there were two minutes left.

Chris sprinted up to her, eyes wide behind his Zorro mask. "Did you kill him?" he asked, voice trembling.

"I don't know. But we gotta go. He might try to get up again."

As they turned to leave, Lucy felt a tug. Looking down, she noticed the werewolf man was still lying there but his right hand had grabbed a hold of her long skirt. His chest was no longer rising and falling. He was deathly still.

"Go without me. I'll get my skirt unstuck and follow you. Run just in case!" She pushed him away toward the front door.

"But—"

"Go!" Lucy yelled, tugging on her plaid skirt.

Twisting and jerking the fabric did nothing. She was caught by a dead man.

You're a murderer, Lucy. You can't make this worse now. He's already dead!

After a moment of hesitation, she once again raised the fire extinguisher above her head and slammed it down on the fist holding her captive. She could hear the small finger bones splinter and crack on impact, but she was free.

But should she take a look at his face? Just in case he wasn't dead and needed to be reported, she should be able to describe him. Tentatively, she crouched next to the still man's head. She dug her shaking hands under the mask's opening around his warm neck and peeled it upwards. It stuck in places and ran with blood, slicking her fingers. He was white, in his forties, and his brain was peeking through the front of his skull where the fire extinguisher had pulverized the bone.

Vomit threatened to surge up her throat at the sight. Her vision darkened for a second, then came back to hyper focus on the slightly pulsing gray matter.

She fled, not looking back.

At the neighbor's house she tried to console Chris and wait out the last minute for the police to arrive, but her mind wouldn't leave her alone. *Murderer, murderer, murderer* echoed in her thoughts along with the looping sounds of breaking bones and sight of gore. *You could have just incapacitated him, not stoved his brains out.*

She was a killer, and he would haunt her nightmares for years, but they would live to see another Halloween.

Butcher in the Dark

Pop. THE LIGHTS GO OUT with a final spark of illumination. You stay frozen in place, cleaver in hand, partially butchered meat on the slab in front of you.

Your senses heighten. The cloying smell of congealed blood wafts up from the floor where the runoff will be taken care of later. The only sound is your heartbeat in your ears.

Your nose itches. Nervously, you raise your hand to scratch, realizing only too late the state you're in. The slick blood on your latex-covered hand smears across your face, turning your stomach.

Movement. You turn to peer in the darkness, straining your eyes until they burn. A smile leers back, teeth reflecting the small red light of a recording camera. They lunge.

Decisions

THE SWINGING BARE BULB TRIED its best to illuminate the dingy garage workshop. Investigator Elaine took a deep breath, smelling the bleach, quicklime, and rot. Ceiling beams sagged, termites having made Swiss cheese out of the woodwork.

Her partner was busy securing the location, setting up caution tape. She could take this time to investigate away from the newbie. A piece of paper specked with red sticking out from under a toolbox caught her eye, the only hint of blood in the whole room.

It was a list with about half the names crossed off, a bloody thumbprint over each black strikethrough, sealing the dead victims fates. Elaine read through them carefully.

Adam Gustave
Sophie Sinclair
Pete Sanchez
Dimitri Nikiforov
Alexander Jones
Nathaniel Davies
Boris Brusnikin

The blood over Adam's name seemed the most aged, while Dimitri's was still fairly fresh. All four were known victims of the South Side Strangler. All seven were terrible humans in their own right. Men and women who had crossed the line and done vile deeds hidden from the press. Now, the line had crossed them.

Oh, the dilemma: give security details to those remaining on the marked piece of paper, or give the details of the security to the penner of death.

Decisions.

Giraffe

I ALWAYS WANTED TO BE a giraffe. To be tall enough to able to reach the magical popcorn on the apricot tree. To have a long purple tongue able to taste rainbows.

That was, until that one particular night. The night being short saved my life. Since then, I've wanted to be a turtle. Not friendly and outgoing, like the super tall mammals, but instead having a hard shell to feel secure in. Safe. A place I could tuck my arms, legs, and head inside. As warm inside as a cocoon of blankets knit by Mother. Just roomy enough where I could have tea parties by myself. Away from the man the court deemed innocent. The man who spied on me through my bedroom window and tried to reach in and grab me, my flyaway hairs brushing his grasping hand. Too short.

His nasty breath and stained fingers were imprinted in my memory. As were my mother's terrified yells when she walked in on me and my longtime friend of the window who needed to brush his teeth. I've never had another friend since.

I am a turtle. Not a giraffe.

Lungs

Miniscule bubbles embrace your paling face after slipping through your purpling lips. Your lungs burn with the swelling dread of not knowing if the tumultuous current will ever release you. The floor is up, the cresting wave down, your mind inside out. A slithering vine of kelp wraps around your flailing ankle, anchoring you to your grave. You never meant to die here.

Your hands scramble for the slimy tendril, numb fingers slipping as your head dashes against the rocky ocean floor, rivulets of red mixing in the stinging torrential brine. Large bubbles stream from your slack jaw. Now your lungs burn with salt.

Scarecrow

(Published on Black Hare Press's Patreon, April 26, 2022)

WIND WHIPS THROUGH MY TATTERED, crow-picked shirt, swirling the scents of rotten corn and spilled blood. The shrieking squeals of the now slaughtered pigs echo through my straw-stuffed head.

They are on the prowl. Pigs done, now onto the workers who will not be missed.

Scuffling feet flee through my sparse, dead field. I overlook the stalkers hunting their prey. Creeping. Crouching. Catapulting over obstacles. A farmhand tumbles into the base of my wooden spine. Calloused hands grip me for support, hauling themselves up, ready to sprint.

Bang.

Scarlet wetness spreads across me. Human meat ready to be dressed.

ANGELS AND DEMONS

The Color of Salt

SHE HAD NEVER NOTICED THE color of salt before. Or rather, its color-bending properties. Like blotched watercolor, only more fractal in its drawing of the tints and hues into itself. Becoming whatever was around it. Invisible, except for its unnatural, uncanny qualities. A face not quite right. Eyes bleeding into the skin tones around them, then sucked back into the pinpricks of salty pupils. A person possessed; their soul, their very essence mixing with another inhuman one. A demon trying to hide in a mortal but not quite getting it right. Those people left a faint smell of brimstone in their wake.

Next, she noticed the color of sugar. It acted like salt at first glance, but the fractals on the faces multiplied the eyes in frightening ways, rings and spirals of them ebbing from the bloodshot whites of the human's own. Unknowable angelic beings possessing mere mortals for their hunt. The smell of ozone mixed with a not-quite-placeable sweetness followed those individuals.

Time passed, the strange smells wafting around her more frequently, those strange features swimming on more and more faces. Strangers and family succumbed to the mixing. One by one. Her mother's brown eyes muddied, the light within dimming, the last to be overtaken.

She cried.

As one, every painted eye turned to her. Converged on her.

Flash!

The intoxicating smell of bread assaulted her so strongly she could hear its atoms steaming. So hot it must have just escaped the crucible of a brazen bull.

Light burned through her, melting her consciousness like dripping, saturated paint in water. Twirling smoke swirls of thought and memory, preferences and imagination suspended in blindingly clear liquid. Bleached and burned away. Eradicating her. Making room for the third type of being.

The salt and sugar fled.

Communion

PEOPLE LINE UP FOR COMMUNION, reverent and contrite. Holy wafers dissolve on tongue, the transubstantiation cleansing them all. The wine is offered next, priest partaking last. One by one, they all drink the watered-down concoction. Throats close and souls ascend. All but the priest's disembodied ghost. A poisoner cursed to haunt the church. Pay his penance, and play the organ.

Slit Pipes

EBONY AND IVORY ARE NEVER meant to be played by the hands of the dead. Hands of coalesced ectoplasm dance along the length of the organ, coaxing the most haunting of tunes screaming from the slit throats of the pipes. The pain of the damned pour through those fingers, minor arpeggios offset by the angelic descants of what might have been. Dissonant melodies, like grating chains, set teeth on edge. Nuns cross themselves when they hear the music float through the air from the rectory. They know what fate awaits them, should they poison the communion wine.

Last Photograph

THE SHINY MODEL T PEELED away from the curb, leaving Jack Pole at the doorstep of the old gothic mansion. It was a spectacle to behold, an immaculate beacon of the past standing out among the cookie-cutter homes that lined the rest of the street.

Jack picked up his conditioned leather case of expensive camera equipment, popped his black peacoat collar against the wind, and shuffled down the green hedged pathway. Not a single dandelion was to be seen in the immaculately kept gardens on either side, as if even they feared to tread here. Statues stared at him with following, judgmental eyes.

You know better than to come here, Jack, echoed a familiar voice in his consciousness.

The ornate double doors came into view as the pathway turned a corner. Large and white, they exuded cold as if carved from an iceberg magically held in stasis. They chilled his knuckles as he rapped quickly on their newly repainted surface, the knocks reverberating into the house beyond.

Snick. The doors unlatched from the inside and swung open, revealing a maid dressed in the old ways. All black and white, frills contained to the apron. She moved mechanically, offering to take his hat and coat, as if this was all her days consisted of—waiting upon those unfortunate enough to be asked to visit this infamous estate. The home rumors swirled about.

"This way to the parlor, sir," she intoned, leading him through one of the many offshoots of the grand hall.

The high-ceilinged hallways were candlelit where the light of the outside world could not pierce through. Slow breezes emanated from places unknown, picking at his bare wrists. If he were a poet, there would be enough atmosphere in this house to inspire dreary sonnets for a lifetime.

The heavy wooden doors to the parlor groaned open, tendrils of incense sweeping out of the room to twirl in Jack's face with their musty scent. As Jack's boot crossed the threshold, a feeling of absolute dread washed over his skin, sinking into his very soul.

You've walked over your own grave, his deceased grandmother's voice whispered at the back of his mind. Was she here now? Warning him?

"Welcome, Mr. Pole."

The gravelly words broke the spell. The hairs on the back of Jack's neck stayed standing, however, bearing witness that the incident had been real.

He looked around the large, dimly lit room to find the speaker. All the windows were shuttered and drapes were over what he assumed to be mirrors. Six people were seated at a round table with candles, incense, herbs, and other trinkets scattered atop it. The rotund elderly man of the group was hoisting himself out of his seat.

Jack nodded somberly to the rising gentleman. "Yes, Mr. Dawson. I'm here for the séance. However, I feel the need to impress upon you that this is a very bad idea. I can feel it. Something is going to go wrong."

Mr. Dawson slowly ushered Jack to his appointed place in the draped corner of the room. "Nonsense, my dear boy. It's just the nerves. The spiritual medium will be here any second. She is of high renown. You will not be participating, but merely observing and documenting through those glorious pictures of yours. I hope they live up to your reputation."

Jack had fought hard for that reputation. There was no way he was going to tarnish it now. "You're right," he said, steeling himself. "It's just the nerves."

Mr. Dawson shuffled unsteadily back to his velvet upholstered seat at the table and resumed his position.

The candles dimmed, flickering almost to being snuffed out as the doors opened once again, revealing a woman wearing a voluminous black dress and long transparent black veil nearly dragging on the polished wooden floor.

"I'm Mrs. Blackwell," she announced, sweeping up to the table in the center of the parlor, owning the room with her presence. "Shall we begin?"

The hairs on the back of Jack's neck prickled once again as an invisible finger traced his nape, just as his grandmother had done to him while he was a child. He missed her.

"I don't think—" Jack was cut off by her fiery glare. Cowed, he finished setting up his camera and silver-coated plates to capture the photographs in silence. Maybe since he wasn't participating, he would be fine.

The circle was formed, hands clasped all around the table. The shadows the candles cast took on a more ominous dance, their depths hinting at a deeper darkness about to unfold.

Mrs. Blackwell cleared her throat, then stared at each person at the table in turn. "Whatever happens, do not break the circle." She bowed her head and closed her veiled eyes. "I call upon the spirits within the sound of my voice." Mrs. Blackwell's voice was ethereal, yet it held the confidence of decades of practice. "Give us a sign by ringing this bell."

Jack relaxed as she continued to ask for the impossible. Maybe nothing would happen. Maybe he was nervous for nothing.

Tick. Tick. Tick. Jack's pocket watch kept him aware of the slow passage of empty time. Time where nothing unexplained happened. Time of getting paid to do nothing but sit and stare.

Ring. Ring.

Fear crashed up Jack's spine. It was really happening.

Flash! He took a picture of the ornate silver bell upon the table, wishing he could capture sound as well. Jack couldn't tell if it was levitating or not. He'd have to wait until after he'd developed the photos.

Flash! A bubbling stream of ectoplasm oozed from Mrs. Blackwell's mouth, through her mesh veil, to hang in midair over the center of the table.

Flash! The torso of a man in uniform coalesced from the viscus black substance, his pale eyes wide and mouth twisted in a dying scream.

Whoosh . . . Complete darkness, the candles whipping into extinction. Jack gripped his grandmother's crucifix in his pocket and prayed to her, his patron saint. Was she still here with him?

Flash! Jack set off another bulb to photograph whatever was coming through now. In the explosion of light, he could see a red hand reaching up the phantom man's face, dragging it back down into the stream of ectoplasm. The smell of fire and brimstone filled the room with suffocating intensity. Ash gritted in his teeth.

Flash! The upper half of a demon crawled out of the black boiling stream. Its acrid orange and yellow eyes were slit like a goat's, the face they were sunken into as smooth and chubby as a toddler's. The arms were the length of a man's, fingers as long and sharp as spindles. The body, however, was an ever-twisting mist of suspended blood droplets, their metallic smell mixing with the brimstone.

The high-pitched scream of a woman filled the air, growing wet and hoarse after a few seconds. Jack switched the glass plates out of the camera as fast as his shaking fingers would allow.

Flash! The long thin arm of the abomination held Mrs. Blackwell's still-moving tongue aloft, blood dripping into its open mouth, sliding down its childlike throat, where it re-emerged to join the other droplets in its wraithlike body.

All humans present shrieked and cried, a raucous laughter tainting the sounds with demonic pleasure. The circle broke as the participants fled to the doors, tripping and piling up on one another in their haste, trampling Mr. Dawson, leaving him to gurgle in the blood of his crushed windpipe.

Jack was down to his last bulb and plate. The last impression he would make in his lifetime. He unraveled the long wire of the clicker and moved in front of the camera.

Flash! Light exploded around him.

Jack Pole imagined the composition as he felt a fatal bloody red hand be yanked from his chest as he kneeled center frame. Soft glowing feathers brushed either side of his face. The resplendent wings of his saintly grandmother framed him as she came to take him with her. Save his soul. The writhing demon was crushed beneath her feet, defeated by the heel of her love.

Reunited at last, they ascended.

Damned

HIS EYES GLOW WITH THE fires of hell. He opens his jaw wide, consuming the pitiful humans. Arms rip and flesh tears asunder under his powerful tombstone teeth, each the size of a mountain. The names of the devoured etch upon the enamel, joining the list of the damned. Those pathetic enough murder in cold blood are reaped for justice. Eaten for revenge.

The Witches Purge

"GUILTY," STATED THE JUDGE, HIS ancient powdered wig a symbol of his righteous benevolence in the colonial god-fearing village. He had just listened to the fervent testimonies of many of the inhabitants. Upstanding citizens, the lot of them, unlike the pitiful creature being accused today. She was from the edge of town, an outcast single mother living off the barren land. The only person who could not even afford a winter-worthy cloak in the changing seasons.

"No! I'm not the Witch of Mendes!" cried the woman, her face red and splotchy from weeping, legs branded from hot irons and arms lanced by needles. "They're all lying! I saw Mr. Brigham kill those sheep myself!" Her words were slightly slurred from her probable concussion and newly missing front tooth.

"The sentence is burning at the stake. Take her now."

The poor shrieking soul was dragged away to the village square where a monstrous pyre had already been erected. Her fate had been irrevocably sealed once the accusation had been made.

A spark lit the fire, which grew ever higher. One little boy cried out while being held back by a woman of the village. Acrid smoke swirled in hell patterns, heralding the destination of his mother tied to the smoldering stake. Her screams shredded her throat, the smoke burning the open wounds as the flames licked hungrily around her. The smell of burnt hair and charred meat filled the town square, sweet and terrible.

"It's all right, little one. We'll look after you now," the boy's neighbor who had accused his mother cooed softly. "She's the last. There'll be peace now."

The five-year-old curled into her shoulder, hiccupping between sobs, wrapping his small fingers into her lilac cloak to ground himself. Her spindly fingers raked through his soft dark hair, smearing the fallen ashes of his now deceased mother into his baby locks. Anointing him. He could not see the grin spreading across her face.

The illustrious judge approached the pair, his visage dissolving to show his true form. Cloven hooves emerged from the split in his robes. Curved horns grew from his sloping forehead as his face elongated. Coarse hair sprouted to cover all visible skin as his eyes turned an acrid yellow.

Wings sprouted from his back, shredding the remains of his mortal clothing. The partially human Goat of Mendes. The Devil.

"You are one of us, child. Welcome to the Society." His voice was grating and cracked as if his vocal cords were still shifting. "Your Christian mother was the last to be purged. Our village is now pure." A hairy hand reached out and caressed the small boy's forehead, marking him.

The young orphan screamed in agony and buried his face in the rough cloak of his mother's bringer of death as the mark of the Devil sprang up dark and throbbing against his pale, translucent skin, burning away his infant baptism. A child of prophecy fulfilled.

Gingerly, he took the boy into his arms, releasing the witch to join the festivities. Singing and dancing exploded into existence drowning them in celebration. Long skirts swirled and colorful cloaks fluttered. A great feast was brought out, the sweet smells heady. They were done with stage one. The real work could now commence.

Birth of a Nephilim
(Published in Dark Moments,
Black Hare Press, August 24, 2022)

RACHEL GASPED AS SHE WAS overshadowed by a fallen angel. Her soul dissolved, mingling with one of dark fire and rock. They separated, but she was left changed.

"The baby is too big!" yelled the midwife. "There is no way you can push out something of that size!"

Rachel gritted her teeth. "Then cut it out."

Hot blood splashed the lavish desert tent's cushioned interior as a sharp hunting knife bit into her bulging, deformed taut belly, rending thick layers of bloody membranes in twain. From the deep fissure rose a being with wings hard as stone.

Son. Destroyer. Nephilim.

Childhood Friend

"SANDRA . . . SANDRA . . ."

The voice reverberates through her mind while in the space between sleeping and wakefulness. The tone and youthfulness of the voice all too familiar. *He's back.*

In terror, she sits up, sheets falling to her waist. *No, no, he can't be back.* Sweat slicks her back, the breeze chilling her skin.

She looks around the room from her position in bed. Nothing appears to be behind the nightstand or the comfy chair. The wardrobe is shut, as is the bathroom door.

Carefully, she slips out of bed and creeps to the cheap put-it-together-yourself wardrobe and places her ear to the doors. It's impossible to hear anything over the pounding of her heart in her own ears. *Thump-thump. Thump-thump.*

Bang!

Something inside slams against the closed doors, pushing her away with force. Giggling seeps between the now cracked doors.

Sandra springs to her nightstand and pulls open the top drawer. The rosary is hot to the touch, but she endures it anyway. "Hail Mary, full of grace—"

Boom. The lights go out in time with a clash of thunder.

"Sandra . . . Don't you remember me, Sandra?"

The sound of the filling tub comes muffled from the still-closed bathroom.

Voices from the past echo in her mind.

"You will be baptized! Then the Father will be able to perform the exorcism!" Her hair is drenched as she's dunked head-first into the tub over and over, no time to breathe.

Wait, she's still in her room. That was years ago.

"The Lord is with thee. Blessed art thou among women," she continues with raw, wet vocal cords.

A male's voice now fills the room from the past. "You let him into you! You agreed to be possessed!"

She screams. "No! No, I never!"

"Sandra, behind you."

Sandra whips around, rosary burning fiercely in her grasp, glowing red from the heat, cooking her skin, the smell making her stomach churn.

A dark wind whirls, tangling her hair about her face. Blinding her to the dangers ahead.

The bedroom door opens, straight into her face, knocking her out with a deep gash. The perfect entrance to invade through.

"We'll be good friends once again, Sandra. Forever."

Failed Harvest

THE STUNTED WITHERED STALKS REACH toward the clouds pregnant with past-due rain. I always knew this harvest would be a bust. Ever since the heat came and Evon left me, my luck has turned. The pale band of skin around my finger shines with unnatural translucency, the blood from my sluggish heart somehow still pumping beneath its surface. Visible for all who care to see. Like my grief.

"Your loan can only be extended by one harvest. I'm sorry, but that's the best we can do." The loan officer at the bank shuffles the printed pictures of my fields back into a neat pile, then places them facedown. Probably to hide my suffering. Easier to be heartless that way.

I shamble outside where the blasted sun immediately starts burning into my skin, burning away my hope and logic. Blood boils in my brain. Red taints my vision.

"Ahhhh!" I scream to the sky, beyond caring who hears.

"You know, there's always the crossroads deal."

The raspy voice startles me out of my rage. There, behind me, is a little girl who sounds like a grown man who smokes two packs a day.

"Excuse me?" My voice comes out more venomous than I intend, but I don't care.

"Meet me outside your house, at 300N and 900W, at midnight." The girl's lips don't move as the words are spoken, her eyes staring straight to my soul.

I blink, and she's gone. Nothing but a mirage of haze rising from the baking, melting asphalt of the parking lot.

My blood runs cold, stories from my grandfather rising like ghosts in my mind. A crossroads demon. A sure way to turn my luck around, but only for the long run if I can get the better of it. I wring my fingers together, crushing my knuckles habitually. Only, it feels different this time. No solid gold band is in between them now. Just muscle, tendon, and bone. It's all I'll have left if I don't get a bountiful harvest beyond my dreams next season.

A smile tugs at my lips, plan hatched.

"Pleased to see you again."

The demon is in its true form this time, innumerable red eyes with black sclera twisting around themselves in ribbons floating above the dirt road. Wisps of ozone emanate from the being like burning electricity.

"What do you wish?"

Heart in my throat at the unnatural sight, I pause. *Do I really want to make a deal with something so otherworldly? If it looks like that, surely it can't determine the true value certain things have to humans. The divorce is finalized, anyway.*

"The most plentiful harvest in the whole state every season until the day I die."

A disembodied chuckle floats from the mass of eyes. How it speaks without a mouth is beyond me, but I know better than to question a demon.

"And what will you give to me in exchange?" it asks.

My trembling hand digs into the front pocket of my jeans, pulling out the ring box. I have to clear my throat a few times to unstick it.

"I give to you my marriage." I hold out the open box, well-worn gold wedding band glinting in the moonlight.

"Deal," the demon says immediately. A little too quickly. But my marriage is nulled, shredded, disintegrated beyond repair. The smoke of its wreckage still dissipates in the air.

Within a blink, the creature of nightmares has folded the world around itself, dissolving like paint in acetone. The ring still remains heavy in my hand.

The barley kernels grow plump, the stalks twice the height of my neighbor's own measly crops. A perpetual sparse cloud cover shields my bounty from the worst of the pounding sun's rays. Frequent rain bursts distill like dew over the deep green sheaths.

I hire someone with expressive eyes and full lips to help

drive the combine harvester. We talk on the handheld radios across the fields, then over lunch under the shade of the barn, then over dinners in my humble home. They don't mind I haven't a penny to my name.

Hours pass talking about the strangely amiable weather that seems to end at my property line, about our favorite sports teams, books, food, movies. Then, we sit in silence, enjoying each other's company. They start staying over.

The relationship is beautiful. We don't have to perform to keep each other entertained. We work side by side and hold each other close through the night. I don't tell them of my deal with the crossroads demon. It doesn't matter, anyway. Evon hasn't tried to contact since that day, so the deal is fine. The past is buried.

As the final swaths of barley are brought in, they propose to me. I say yes. Tears of happiness flood my eyes, my tanned finger ready to bear the weight of a new ring.

Church bells ring out after the final bales of barley are sold. Our wedding vows and rings are exchanged.

My new platinum ring dissolves as it's placed on my finger.

Ozone fills the chapel. My beloved blinks, turning away, staggering from the altar. Confusion distorts their beautiful face.

I call out their name with a trembling voice.

"Who are you?" they cry, holding their hands out in defense, keeping me at bay.

I back off, heart aching, and scream to the ceiling. "I meant my old marriage!"

A deep, rasping chuckle bounces off the perfect acoustics. "You never said it in words. And I never took your old ring."

I'm rich and alone, my bed empty and cold. Has been for decades. I thought I'd be happy once the loan officers got off my back. Had enough to buy a bigger barn. Get a private plane. See the world.

I still see my beloved from time to time when I visit the next town over for errands. They cower, immediately crossing the street, no matter how busy, whenever I enter their view. I can't drag them into my cursed existence again despite my aching heart. I tried being in a relationship again with two others, but those affairs were cursed to ruin as well. I may grow crops like gangbusters, but I will never grow love again. That harvest will always fail.

THE SEEPING SUPERNATURAL

Mirror Mirror

Someone's living inside my mirrors. They've studied me intently my entire life. They know how I move, my mannerisms and quirks. They even breathe in time with me. However, I know that's not my reflection. Reflections ripple along surfaces, an imitation of life. Not imbued with life itself.

What it gets up to while I'm sleeping, I'll never know. Cameras fritz and computers die when pointing at my mirrors. Just the ones inside my home. The ones She inhabits.

She keeps looking at me with such disappointment. Grief. Loathing. Fury. Her screams release as her shards go flying.

Imaginary Friend

CLINK! I raise the teacup to hers, then sip at the non-existent tea.

"Where are you from, Ms. Nesbit?" Her childish voice rings through the room stuffed with toys.

I blink back tears, my life still too fresh. Then an idea dawns in my mind. A way to make this sufferable. "I'm sorry, Alex. If I tell you, you'll die like I did."

Her eyes go wide. "You're dead?"

"Oh yes. I'm forced to keep my past life a secret, or you will be cursed."

She does not bring it up again, terrified of the consequence. The days flow in fun. We frolic through daisy fields and make flower crowns.

It's the day before school, where she will make living friends. I am so close to peace and moving on. Then I lose her as well.

Before Alex's blood has even dried on the asphalt near the bus stop, I am in another bedroom.

Clink!

Child

THE CHILD LOOKED UP AT me with wide, innocent eyes. Her dead family surrounded her. The plague. Unbidden, a pang hit my inhuman heart. I would look back on this moment with regret later, but I was drowning in her deep sorrowful eyes rimmed with jaundice. I did the only thing I could think of. My fangs gently pierced her wrist as I partook to initiate the ritual. The black blade gifted me by my sire slid through my own flesh, the blood of eternity welling sluggishly at the wound. She drank. And was cursed forever to the body of a six-year-old. Never to be recognized or considered an adult despite her hundreds of years of experience by my side. And a hundred more away from me, hunting me for revenge.

I deserved it.

Into the Catacombs

LEAVES SWIRLED IN THE NOVEMBER air as Brian Heathcomb turned up his wool coat collar against the wind. He was finally here in Paris on a once-in-a-lifetime visit, far from his cozy, modest countryside home in Durham, England. Even as far north as he originated, word of the catacombs had spread, its walls of bones covering miles of the underground beneath this historic gem of Paris. Bones said to have supernatural properties in the right hands. And as his grandmother Lily had divined, he had the right hands.

The year was 1805. King George III ruled over a vast empire. After all these years and advancement of society the catacombs were still not open to the public. Tonight would be the night he fulfilled his life's dream: find a bone that called to him. He had food, water, twine, and torch supplies in his satchel, enough for all night and the next day, just in case. If only he could find an entrance.

"Vous, monsieur, cherchez-vous à descendre dans les catacombes?"

Brian jumped in fright at the unexpected voice. He'd been so focused on inspecting the walls of the alleyways he had not noted the pale man on the other side of the gate at the end.

"Sorry? I don't speak much French. Did you say catacombs?"

"Oui, les catacombes. I speak little English. You want guide?" The pale man was tall, and his voice was wispy. His dusty older clothes looked like they had recently been exhumed from the catacombs themselves.

"Yes! Oui, oui, Merci." Brian's heart was in his throat. It was his lucky night. Cautiously, he approached the wrought iron gate at the end of the long hidden alleyway.

"Up!" The man gestured.

Anchoring his knee-high leather boots into the wrought iron swirls, Brian scaled and hoisted himself over the ornate fence locked with chains. They would not keep him from his dream.

"Thank you so much for being my guide. My name is Brian Heathcomb. What is your name?"

"Pardon?" the man asked.

Taking a deep breath to quell his excitement and slow his speech, he tried again. "I'm Brian Heathcomb. You?"

"Philibert Aspairt."

The name sounded familiar, but he could not quite put his finger on it. "Philibert? Good to meet you." He held out his hand to shake with the good gentleman, but the pale man only nodded in response, tipping his top hat. Then he turned and led the way to the edge of the walk where a gap in the gutter showed a hole large enough for a man to slide into.

"Are you serious? Is there no bigger opening?" Brian asked. "I might get stuck!"

"I go, you go. Suivez-moi." He stepped down into the gutter and then slid down the hole, his hat disappearing last in a plume of dust.

Brian followed suit, holding his breath as disturbed earth swallowed him. He came out the bottom into a passageway lit by a flaming torch. It seemed to have been lit in anticipation of his arrival. There was a bundle of rags beneath it for continued hours of usage.

"Take fire, follow." The tall man gestured to the only torch before he began to walk into the darkness.

"Wait, shouldn't you take it? Don't you need to see where we're going?" Brian called out. He took out his large ball of twine and tied an end to the torch hook. Then he grabbed the torch and rags, stuffing the extras into his bag before hurrying off to catch up to the receding back of Philibert.

He couldn't believe it. He was here, inside the catacombs. The air was damp and cloying, the change in pressure noticeable to his ears. He could hear water dripping up ahead, but the bowels of the caverns and tunnels seemed eerily silent, like a sound humans could not pick up was vibrating in their depths.

Names were carved into the walls, signs that they were not the first to pass this way. There were no bones, supernatural or mundane, in sight yet, but he knew they were somewhere in here. He was so close now.

Through corridors they walked, hugging sides of the walls at points to sidestep wells and pits. Philibert didn't say a word. Brian was not sure if it was because of the language barrier or if he was just the silent type. He didn't mind, though, as it gave him time to focus on his surroundings. His twine was still trailing behind him, giving him peace.

It was not long into the journey that scurrying noises began to creep into his peripheral hearing. "Are there rats down here?"

"Rats? Oui. And lutin and matagot."

Lutin and matagot. He had never heard of lutin before.

He cursed as a sharp stone entered his left knee-high boot somehow. As quickly as he could he took his shoe off and extracted the shard. Philibert waited on the edge of the light for him.

Once Brian got his boot back on, they trudged down a corridor to the left. Two more rocks entered his right boot this time. He decided to ignore them for as long as possible.

There were many branches to the dusty tunnel. Music flitted through some of them, the sound of guitars and even a hurdy-gurdy mixing in mellow hymns. The locals seemed to enjoy congregating in the outskirts of the catacombs.

Brian's cramped muscles relaxed as they passed those branches. They were not alone. Even if he did get separated from Philibert and his twine he could follow the sound of music to find others and get out with them.

"Careful, water."

Lifting the torch as high as he could in the cramped confines, Brian got to see the flooded passageway.

"Isn't there another way around?" he asked.

"Best way," the older, stooping man said.

The water came halfway up his shins. Ripples in the water made the light of the torch dance, casting eerie shadows up the walls. The slogging sound of his wading seemed to distort into the sounds of distant laughter. Philibert's practiced movements were as silent as the grave. After a quarter of a mile, they emerged from the water and began to continue on muddy ground. The voices echoed around him, leading them onward.

The corridor opened into a vast chamber. People were gathered with torches in the center of the room. They had cloaks with hoods up. Some cloaks were silk and wool, while others were of a doeskin weave. All walks of life were represented. Most were kneeling on the ground except one woman, who was dancing with a ghostly apparition of a woman in white. Those kneeling sang in French in intertwined harmonies, their merriment bouncing off the walls in resounding echoes that took on lives of their own.

"Sorcières," hissed Brian's guide.

"Witches." Brian was entranced. All his life he had heard tales of diverse magic and folklore from his retired medium grandmother. Here it was in front of him, dancing and breathing and so alive.

The witches had summoned one of the Dames Blanches. The dancing witch's cloak swirled as did the skirts of her dress. She seemed to be an aristocrat if the cut and quality of the fabrics were anything to go by. The White Woman ghost was so ethereal and enchanting with her floor-length blond hair and floating folds of her white dress that Brian felt a longing to dance with her himself. If he could only get close enough, he could wait out his turn. He could join with them and learn secret truths.

"Stay back," commanded Philibert.

At his outburst the witches turned to look at who had interrupted their dancing and communion with the spirits. Once they caught sight of the two of them, they shrieked in terror and tore from the chamber. The apparition faded forlornly as their circles broke.

"Il est là, ils viendront," they cried.

"What are they saying? Why are they frightened?" Brian asked his guide, while retreating back to his side. "Was it something I did?"

"No outsiders. Follow."

The translations didn't seem to fit what French he knew, but he didn't press further.

They skirted around the now empty room and into another dark passageway. Bone deposits lined the walls. Brian's hopes soared. They must be entering the actual ossuary part of the catacombs where he could commune with the ancient bones and find one that called back.

The name "Philibert Aspairt" scratched at his subconscious again. Where had he heard it before? Surely it had to do with the catacombs.

Brian's stomach fell to the floor; the twine was no longer taut. Looking back, he saw the back of a large black cat drawing its claws over it.

"Hey! Stop that!" called out Brian. The cat took the end of the detached string and ran off with it. His lifeline was gone.

"What was that damned beast?" he asked Philibert.

"Matagot. Demon cat."

A walker between worlds. They must be close.

"Here." Philibert pointed.

It was an opening just big enough to crawl through. The hole was lined with femurs, ulnas, humeri, and stone. They were here!

"Philibert, you good man. Thank you. I guess I'll go first with the torch?"

"Oui." The tall, thin man gestured to the hole once more.

Taking a deep breath, Brian got on his hands and knees, then shuffled through the hole. The view on the other side took his breath away. Everywhere he looked there were solid walls of bones. Arms and legs were stacked on one another with stripes of skulls breaking up the monotony. There was a stone basin on a pedestal in the center of the room. Brian put a couple rags into it and lit them with the torch. The room brightened, shadows dancing in the empty eye sockets surrounding him. They seemed to be trying to tell him something.

"All my life I have heard of this place. Thank you, dear friend. I will forever be indebted to you for showing me the way."

Turning to look to his guide, Brian noticed he was standing next to a tombstone placed into the wall. Inscribed upon it were the words:

A LA MEMOIRE DE PHILIBERT ASPAIRT PERDU DANS CETTE CARRIERE LE III NOVEMBRE MDC-CXCIII RETROUVE ONZE ANS APRES ET INHUME EN LA MEME PLACE LE XXX AVRIL MDCCCIV

With his basic knowledge of French, Brian was able understand the first part of the inscription: "In Memory of Philibert Aspairt." Recollection rang through him. Philibert Aspairt had gotten lost in the catacombs for eleven years before his bones were found and put into the wall. It had been over a year since his body had been found. He was a dead man.

"Um, Philibert. Are you related to that Philibert?" he asked, pointing to the tombstone.

The pale man just laughed and whistled. It was piercing and rang through the many corridors. A growl answered back.

Brian's blood ran cold, thoughts of magical bones forgotten. Desperately he ran back to the hole and started to climb back through it. His hands were free on the other side when he felt the dreaded snap of teeth on his boot. Mercilessly, something dragged him back toward the room of death. He no longer wanted to be here.

As he looked back, Brian saw what had his foot trapped in its maw. A giant wolfdog. It was at least two meters long. Stories of all the wolf attacks in France and across mainland Europe came back to him. The Beasts of Gévaudan. Over a hundred people slain by these creatures in only three years before they disappeared. Disappeared, or relocated.

The yellow eyes of his attacker glinted in the torch light. The red fur streaked with black was matted with dust. Brian screamed in fright and pain as the jaws clenched even harder around his ankle, grinding his bones together, splintering them. The long teeth pierced through the leather of his shoe, drawing blood.

"Philibert! Help! Please!" he cried. He was being pulled backward out of the hole.

"Seven souls sacrifié, lead to les Bêtes du Gévaudan. Now I free," Philibert said in his ear as he dissolved into vapor around him. The beasts behind him seemed to be chuckling, the one biting his ankle rumbling with mirth.

The torch fell from Brian's grasp on the far side. His fingers cut on the bone fragments lining the wall, smearing blood along them as he grappled for purchase. A mist rose from the bones, forming into ghostly shapes.

He clutched at a skull, but it came free of the ornate pattern of remains.

He chucked it at the wolf creature's head. The wolf gave a snort of surprise and dropped him. Desperately, Brian got up and hobbled as fast as his obliterated ankle would let him, adrenaline numbing his agony to an extent.

The ghostly apparitions he had accidentally summoned charged at the creature, yelling things. All he could manage to translate was "leave" and "alone."

Around the pedestal of flame he went and down into another corridor of bone.

Darkness consumed him. His breathing and the throb of his heartbeat flooding his ears were punctuated only by a howl. With no torch to guide him, all he had was touch and smell to go by.

He needed to get his breathing under control, but he also needed to get away as fast as possible. Dragging his hand along the protruding femurs lining the wall, he made his way deeper into the unknown.

The clatter of wolf nails and panting had stopped at the last turn. His heartbeat stabilized the farther he went as nothing happened. Wind whistled in the distance. An exit to the catacombs. Freedom. It was so near!

Up ahead, a shaft of sunlight beamed down a set of stairs. They illuminated hope and despair, for in the light there was also another giant wolf wearing what looked to be a rotting boar skin for armor. There was nothing he could do.

A deep howl that rumbled through his own bones reverberated down the corridor. Glowing eyes at a man's height stared deep into his own. The stench of the rotting hide washed over him. Brian wished for nothing more than to be at home in his own warm bed under the quilt his grandmother had made.

The Beast of Gévaudan gave a chuckling whuffle. Brian was sure it smelled his fear. He slid the pack over his shoulder and took out all the food he had brought and laid it out at his feet in offering. His only chance. The whuffling increased as his actions amused the creature. He was a dead man. It lunged for his throat.

His scream rang up through the streets of Paris.

Monster of Calumnia

(On the podcast *Tales to Terrify*, March 3, 2023)

THE DESIGNATED LAND FAR FROM any prying town was leveled, all life removed from the once fertile vicinity to make way for Camp Calumnia. Stones were split with the ringing metal pickaxes of those forced to live there. Thin wooden walls erupted from the now barren soil, barely enough to block the biting, howling winds. Pallets of food arrived for those in charge, the boards recycled into bunks for those interred within. Little of the sustenance would be spared for them.

It only took one night for the first shot to ring out. The first cry of the unearthly creature to be heard on the outskirts of the camp.

The scavenging being was small and thin, the size of a toddler, scrounging around on all four emaciated limbs. No eyes glinted in the torch lights. A monster of pure darkness.

As the days drudged on, more shots rang out through the compound. Piles of corpses rose from shallow graves outside the barbed wire fences, testaments to the cruelty of humanity. At night, the sounds of pilfered pockets and broken dreams filled the air. Photographs formerly hidden away, stitched into the seams of peasant clothing, were now freed. Darkened by blood stains, they littered the faces of those who had once held them dear. Left to the whims of the wind.

Skritch. Skritch.

The fast-growing, hunched scavenging creature scrambled over the maggot-ridden piles, picking at the open wounds left by the supposed caretakers. With each rattling breath, it consumed the dark miasma emanating from the evidence of torture. Each lungful caused its limbs to lengthen, torso to deepen with shadows, and broken nails to extend with jagged cracks.

After a few years, word got around of the Monster of Calumnia. Human eyes would peer into the darkness of starless nights, wondering if each rasping sound was a herald of damnation. Those interred thought of it as a personification of their own suffering, while others deemed it something summoned by the blackest of magics only the interred folk knew. They would need to starve the possible magic out of the inmates faster.

For six long years, the camp continued. Years of mutilation, death, and unspeakable atrocities. Years for the frontline to encroach upon the camp's borders.

Whoosh! The flames set by the wardens licked hot and fierce out of the glassless windows of buildings unlucky entombed souls were locked in. Trapped by the hot metal bars, the palms of their hands melted with each grasp toward freedom. The raid sirens pierced their overwhelmed ears, the liberators on their way.

But not fast enough.

With their dying screams carried on the wind, the sun fell below the red horizon obscured by smoke and the smell of burnt bodies.

The creature could take no more.

A bellow as deep as the pits of hell and as gravelly as brimstone echoed over the camp. The Monster of Calumnia would stand by no longer as the people whose suffering he'd spawned from perished. Lunging on its elongated feet, its nails gripped the charred soil, and it sprinted to the main plaza.

Gasps of the dying and healthy onlookers alike filled the air as the creature of pain and anguish was revealed in full at last. Harsh spotlights flooded the courtyard, their blue tints illuminating the gauze-wrapped head streaked with crimson. Its appendages had multiplied, as had its enormous size. As large as a tank and as fierce as an oppressed nation, all six arms reached farther than seemed possible. Those appendages seized the weaponry mounted on the observation towers, wrenching them, twisting them from their bolted seats of power.

As those consigned to the flames grew deathly quiet, the monster expanded. Shadows licked from its sides, swiping swaths of men off their feet. Plucking the sight from their eyes, it left their final vision the consequences of their own doing.

Flames dwindled to embers, the scattered ashes dancing across the scorched soil, blessing it to give way to life in the future with their final sacrifice.

The liberators rolled into the camp, only to see the twisted remains of molten metal and splintered, smoldering wood. Reconnaissance teams sifted through the debris to find the lone survivor—a six-year-old boy.

A dirty six-year-old with a face bandaged with red wrappings, whose raw eyes did not reflect in the torch light.

Innards

SQUEAK.

The telekinetic cat grinned. Pushing things off shelves had lost its charm. Pulling organs out of mice, however, was delightful.

The glistening intestines hung in midair next to the spinning, beating heart. They were, however, small. The cat wondered how large the pulsing innards of his humans were.

Scream.

Nourish Me

THE GNARLED KNOTS ARE MY eyes, the twisted branches my arms, the reaching roots my seat. I speak through the eloquent wind, cry through the torrential rain, and whisper through the suspended dust motes. I am the forest.

The blood of men runs down my vines, enriching my soil for the vegetation. Their brains rot, exposed to my air to feed my insects. Desolate bodies decay in my undergrowth to fatten my animals.

Forward I call them. Humans to nature. Souls to spirit. They bestow themselves to sustain me.

My borders expand. My ecosystems flourish.

Nourish me as I rise.

Headless Horseman

THE SPY PARTS FROM HIS lover, she to return to her home in the woods, and he to find Commander Wilhelm Von Knyphausen with intel to win the war received.

"I'll return once the war is won, dear Anabel. Your service has placed you under our protection. Wait for me at the large old oak in the forest in two weeks' time, my love." He swoops into the saddle of his trusty stallion, cape fluttering around him to conceal his Hessian uniform from the locals.

Forward he charges, dashing through the small-town Sleepy Hollow. Down the main road and toward the battlefield. Villagers hunker down in their homes, windows shut and sealed.

The open battle plains of New York spread before him, the earth pockmarked from the flint hooves of sweating cavalry and the impacts of cannons.

Boom. Sky and ground swirl, end over end in chaos. His eardrums explode, drowning out the cries of fellow Hessian soldiers and the death scream of his horse.

Moonlight caresses the unconsecrated soil of the pauper's grave next to the churchyard, illuminating where the head of the dead man should be as he is laid to rest. The brutally charred remains of a neck poke out the yellow collar of his uniform. None of the Americans mourn the passing of the Hessian. They don't even know his name, except for Anabel, who waits too long in the forest, driven from her home by a mob. She coughs wetly as the snow falls.

She succumbs, now the woman in white, wailing among the trees.

Skeletal hands of the trees cast jagged shadows from the full moon across the packed earth of the mass grave no one attends to. Now, he will visit them.

The banshee screams of Anabel echo across the road, reaching the ears of the dead. Lightning strikes the slab of a tombstone.

Crack!

Rubble explodes as the stone splits down the middle. Horse hooves stomp, leaving imprints in the freshly exposed soil above the interred. Booted feet slide into stirrups.

The headless horseman rides.

Sparks fly from the shoed hooves of the revenant steed. His rider leans low, charred neck exposed. The call of his love draws him down the main thoroughfare and deep into the woods. Branches clutch at his cape and uniform caked in unhallowed dirt.

The unearthly screech calls once again. He calls to her through supernatural means, his deep voice echoing through the thick trunks.

"Anabel," he calls. The vegetation parts.

Her ghostly body, draped in flowing white, floats in the clearing above the snow-capped ground. She flickers, movement jerky, going backward through time. She is running in reverse, out of the clearing and into the woods, inhaling her screams. Back to the village edge she goes, crying the mayor's name among her desperate pleading. Then she is forward again, running into the dead meadow and falling, lying on the ground, snow covering her as she stills.

Over and over she repeats. His voice cannot reach her.

The pit of his stomach fills with the hot burning of molten lead. The mayor and any villagers involved will pay for their cruelty. He will go to his commander, relay the message, and return with a battalion of men to mow down these cretins.

Jerking the reins, he spurs his horse onward to where the battle was raging. The battle he must have died in if his lack of a head is any indication.

Onward they galloped, whipping around the curves in the main road where windows were shuttered, hiding the inhabitants momentarily from his wrath.

The battlefield is barren. No commander tents in sight. Had they lost?

Up the coast he rides, checking the strongholds along the way. Not a British soldier in sight. The Hessian command gone.

At last, he comes upon the main landing docks. Not a single ship is in sight that bears a friendly flag.

A passing insomniac walks drunkenly, whistling in the dark.

Answers.

The Hessian gallops to him, cape flying behind. He draws his wicked sword and pins the quivering man to a wall, point driven through his shoulder.

"Where are the mercenaries?" he asks, voice rumbling through the air between them.

The man lets out a scream of terror, urine running down his legs and into his leather boots.

"The Hessians?" the headless horseman demands again. "Where have they gone?" He drags the sword down, carving from the collarbone to the frantically beating heart.

"Th-they were left behind. Weeks ago. I think they scattered to save their skins."

The British reneged on their promise. The spineless red coats.

He pushes on the hilt, slowly piercing deeper into the pinned swine of a man. Blood wells from the wound and the man moans, red dripping down the dirty tunic and staining it.

They are gone. They lost. His message is useless, and his love is dead for nothing.

In a rage, he dissolves as the first rays of morning sun falls upon him. He will rise again at sunset. This he swears.

The stars hide their faces as the Hessian rises from the grave once more. This time, to take heads as he had lost his own, in the hope it will put his beloved Anabel to rest through well-deserved revenge.

His first target—the mayor of Sleepy Hollow.

The large house of fine workmanship looms large over its fields. The shutters are open, far enough away the baleful cries of Anabel do not reach them. The breeze it allows inside will instead carry their owner's screams.

Crash! He charges on his horse through the front door, smashing it off its hinges.

Once inside, he dismounts, cape billowing behind as he makes his way to the master bedroom. The man and wife clutch at each other, half under the covers, faces white and bloodless.

"In the name of God—" the fat mayor starts to yell, but the slash of the Hessian's sword sends his head flying across the room, mouth still flapping soundlessly. It bounces off the wall, leaving a splat of gore on the imported wallpaper, forever staining it. Spinal fluid mixes with blood and saliva, seeping through the floorboards, forever staining them.

The Hessian leaves the screaming wife, job done for the night.

The next night, after the crops are finished being pickled and preserved and the meat salted, the town gathers for a meeting in the largest barn. The dead mayor's barn.

"What do you mean, the man was headless?" barks the blacksmith. "Was his head covered to protect his identity?"

The crying wife vehemently shakes her head. "No! I saw the stump of his neck!"

"She's just traumatized. In hysterics," another villager says.

The Hessian bides the minutes, listening to them talk. Seeing who respected whom. Weeding out the innocent from the mob. Remembering all the details of these people's lives he was gossiped to in life by Anabel.

Seven men in the corner congregate among themselves.

He locks the doors from outside and glides around the barn to their corner to listen in through the walls.

"If we pretend to be this headless horseman, surely we can take out Mrs. Baas, then the old mayor's belongings will be up for grabs. Too bad there wasn't much in that little Anabel's place. Slim pickings."

Bingo.

His revenant stallion rears on its hind legs, front hooves smashing through the wooden walls of the crowded barn. The horseman wields his sword aloft and brings it down on one of the evil men's necks, parting him from his head.

Everyone present screams and tries to flee but ends up piling upon one another at the barred doors. Torches topple, landing in strewn straw, igniting the nightmare.

One by one, the seven men are decapitated while those who keep their wits shimmy through the busted opening the headless horseman made when entering.

The fire rages on, consuming the wealth of the complicit mayor and those too fearful to use logic. Justice is served. But is it enough?

He flies on his stallion back to the woods, to his beloved.

Silence greets him. Then, the unholy shrieking commences. She is still bound.

Despair drives like a dagger through his phantom heart. Are there others who still need to be dispatched? He will kill them all, one by one if he must. She will be put to rest.

The spurs of his unearthly boots dig into his mount.

The hunt is on.

Planting Hope

POKE. POKE. TINY FINGERS INDENT into wet soil, making neat rows for planting.

Plop. Plop. Bright candy corns are placed in each hole.

Pat. Pat. The child's hand covers them over.

Drip. Drip. A minuscule watering can irrigate them with anticipation.

Watch.

Hope.

Pray.

Wrench. Snap. Broken chicken feathers stick to little hands.

Stab. Slash. Blood glistens, fertilizing the soil.

Rake. Scrape. Wet red mixes with brown.

Stare.

Despair.

Curse.

Wrench. Snap. A mother's bleached blond hair tangles between growing fingers.

Stab. Slash. Blood glistens, fertilizing the soil with even more potency.

Rake. Scrape. Wet red mixes with brown.

Sprout.

Lunar Child

I RAN TO THE OPEN cabin window, desperate to lock it. *Slam!* It shut, the blown glass panes shivering in their latices. With a shaking hand, I jabbed the old rusty lock into place and checked that it was secure. No snow would be coming through it tonight.

I sprinted to the door of my one-room home to lock myself outside. *Smash!* The single knot in the wooden floor halfway to the door caught my shoe for the first time in my life. I sprawled across the floor for only a second, but it was too late. The scar on my leg from the turning bite stood out harsh despite my growing brown fur. My skin rippled and tugged, bones shifting, cracking, realigning. An agonized scream ripped through my throat, but it morphed with my transforming vocal cords into a howl of misery. My baby daughter was next to me, vulnerable.

The small cheery flames of the fire in the grate helped me to blank my mind through the worst of it. Their dance hypnotized my fading humanity. By the time I was conscious again, the fire was but coals being smothered by tiny dancing drifts of snow coming though the still-open doorway.

Eat, must eat, flooded my mind in a never-ending cycle.

My guts roiled and cramped, whether from hunger or still shifting I did not care. A succulent smell reached my elongated nostrils as the spasms slowed into manageable contractions and the pain was pushed to the back of my animal mind. Gingerly, I got up on all fours. My sprained ankle was fixed, fit for the hunt.

Following a sweet scent, my eyes were brought to a human child. *My child.* The idea was fleeting. As a creature of the night, human thought processes were hard.

Slowly I crept up on the baby girl in her soft embroidered dress so as not to spook her. The smell from close up was intoxicating. Saliva gathered unconsciously in my mouth and dripped to the floor.

Splat. Splat.

I nuzzled the arm of the child. Her skin was so smooth and soft, baby fat making her plump. Her shrieks of delight pierced my ears, making my hackles rise in instinct, teeth bared.

A howl broke through the night—another werewolf. I scrambled to heed his call, the need to obey my maker overpowering the need to satiate my hunger. Through the open door I dashed, around deep snow drifts and into the woods, leaving my forgotten daughter to the mercy of the elements and dropping temperatures.

Skeleton Man

MY FEET DRAG ALONG THE scorched sandy expanse, sharp rocks tearing at my translucent skin. The river of recently discovered blood trails my wake, the color enough to cause my stomach to roil. A clear way for the dogs to track me down, if they should even make it this far into the desolate realm. Orange haze engulfs me as the towers of the abandoned City of Cathedrals wink on the horizon. My final resting place. Sanctuary.

Between the rugged cracks of the baked tan land, pulsing veins pull lifeblood toward the city even Death could not kill. Veins that bulged blackish-green and thick are the only sign of life within miles.

It's your fault. You brought color into our world. Color. Differences. War. I grimace as the suspended sand grits in my teeth. I deserve it. The taste of the ashes, my fellow comrades, taint my tongue, coating it with my regret. *Gernard. Samwin. Elizabet.*

Forward I trudge, no longer looking forward to my demise. What will they say when they see me in the spirit plane? Unwelcome. That's what I'll be. Banished. Again.

The looming towers of the organic cathedrals cast long shadows, cutting through the ginger atmosphere, casting me in the reds of my future. Blood droplets will rise from my pours in sacrifice for my misdeeds when I lay myself across the altar of Hrafn. It won't be enough.

At last, I arrive at the city. The blue churches on the left throb in time with each other, sending out their plasma to the great beyond I have just traversed. On the right, yellow buildings crumble, yet seem to be smoldering. Embanked embers deep within threaten to revive should I foolishly enter.

I meander between the buildings, following the knotted pit in my stomach to find the destined structure. The closer I come, the hollower my insides get. Their ache is a sure compass. As the deepest shadow engulfs my thin body, the purple of dead lips tints my skin. A promise.

Spider-like veins weave together, forming the facade of the Cathedral of Hrafn. The most put-together building left by the sands of time.

The doors open wide of their own accord as I drag my rooted feet across the breathing threshold. Tepid, musty air washes over me, pooling in my lungs, its potent neurotoxin pulling me into a state of calm.

"What is it you wish to hear?"

The voice of bone-on-bone grates into my ears. Mustering my strength, my head rises to seek the hollow sockets of the skeleton man at the altar. His leathered skin is pulled taut over protruding angles sharp enough to cut. He is leaning on a withered staff of petrified wood as old as he might be.

Without waiting for a reply, his ancient form moves. Creaks. Scrapes forward, around the beating altar where the heart of the city is laid bare.

Inch by inch, he scritches closer as my limbs grow numb. I'm unable to move, rooted like a succulent meal recently devoured. Digesting in the acidic juices until nothing remains.

The skeleton man raises his staff and points his spindle fingers at me.

I know what he will say before the words escape his toothy grin. The pronouncement kills me all the same.

"Color never existed. It was all just a test."

His words lift the veil covering the retinas of my mind. Oranges, reds, and all the rest fall away. We are nothing but gray.

The Colors

THE COLORS WERE A STRANGE family, as far as the townsfolk of suburbia were concerned. They were obsessed with their namesake, wearing clashing fabrics, painting murals on the walls, and planting foreign flowers all around their cookie-cutter house. Some vegetation smelled of rotting meat to attract scurrying creatures. Police had been called once because Mrs. Azalea was convinced a child had fallen into the carnivorous bulging plant and died.

That wasn't the worst of it.

Since they'd moved in, the colors of shadows had changed. No longer were they a deep navy at all times, but they had shifted to maroons, glowing ambers, and the pale lilac of dead lips.

Some said the family could watch through the shadows. Others said the family could walk through them like wraiths from one cast shadow through to another.

All we knew was the shadows returned to normal once we burned their house down.

With them in it.

Changing

YOU FEEL YOURSELF BECOMING A monster. Legs elongating, extra limbs sprouting, innards melting into gelatinous pools, but you don't mind. Looks are only skin deep, and your skin is now more plasma than human. After all, you still have your mind.

"I love you," you whisper to your hamster. He takes sunflower seeds from your dexterous nails and stuffs them into his grateful cheeks.

"I love you," you tell him as you gaze at his meaty little body, fattening him up on carrots and broccoli.

"I love you," you say as you guzzle him down like Jell-O.

"I miss you."

Soul Eater

(Orla Hart's *Authortube Audiobook Anthology*: Vol. 2)

IT ALL STARTS WHEN I lose my front tooth. The pristine porcelain is hollow and rotted from the inside, dark sludge oozing from where the roots should be. My dentist says it must have been a cavity and to floss more. A new voice inside my head laughs at my tears.

Over the next few weeks my teeth continue to loosen and fall out, one by one. My gums shrink and recede, red and blotchy, festering.

Is this your fault? Why is this happening to me? I think hard while I sob.

You were there when I needed a host. Just random happenstance, it chuckles back. *You should feel honored.*

I see a shrink who puts me on meds, but they do nothing so I stop taking them and ghost her calls. I eat liquids, but after a month even they cannot satisfy the new hunger growing inside me.

You will feast soon enough, echoes the now familiar voice in my brain.

The air crisp with winter holds new scents to me. Every time I pass someone bundled in their coats and scarves, a hint of something sweet wafts over me. Fresh baked bread pales in comparison to the allure of these people.

Breathe it in, my pet. All in good time.

When passing the gym, the smell of human sweat fills the air, turning my stomach. Some people's body odor is rank, yet that sweet allure still floats on top of it. I am hungry for them, but not their bodies.

Bodies decay. Not worth consuming. The words slither up my spine.

A pain grows in my mouth over a few days as a large bridge of something hard replaces where my human teeth had been in my top and bottom plates. It is sharp and a yellow ivory color, growing larger and fuller as the days progress. I can no longer go outside without being stared at, their beady eyes burning into me. I curse the voice in my head but am resigned to my fate at his point.

A fully developed beak stretches my jaw wide and splits my lips into ragged strips to make room. My nose recedes into my skull, nostrils wide. My eyes sink deep into their sockets, a red film covers my vision, the world darkening. Skin slackens as my muscles wane, yet I am stronger than ever.

The heady sweet smell is no longer resistible. I crack open the front door of my studio apartment. The moonlight caresses the landscape in red silhouettes, the world macabre. Down past the parking lot, the forest meets civilization. My blood sings in my ears. *Home.*

My long thin limbs launch me over the railing, bypassing the stairs, straight down four flights. I land in a crouch, my splayed bare feet catching my light weight on the cement sidewalk. The smell of decaying plant life in the undergrowth washes over me as I run on all fours, fingers and toes like claws digging into the good earth for purchase. Light filters through the canopy in irregular patterns, animated by the wind. Carried with it is the sweet scent of human something.

There, among the lower boughs of ancient trees, a man stands talking to a woman. Their aggressive words increase in tempo and volume. I shouldn't go to them. They are just people.

But people's souls are so delicious, comes the luscious voice from within my transformed head.

Souls. That's what I smell. The immortal souls of humans.

A predatory scream tears through my throat, ravaging my shifted vocal cords. An all-consuming hunger washing over my brain, drowning the humanity.

Devour.

The command is the trigger to release my tightly wound muscles as I spring forward, beak wide, homing in on the source of the sickly-sweet vapor now visible to my veiled eyes. It glows brighter than a searchlight and emanates from the area of their stomach, above their navel.

Strike. Snap. Twist.

I gouge my beak deep into the guts of the man around the glowing entity that is his soul. The vapor solidifies at my touch. I shake my head, turning it this way and that to break the ethereal bindings. An unholy shriek from the spirit rings in my ears, fueling on my animalistic death roll, my whole body spinning in midair to jerk the soul from its seat. Blood oozes down my face and splatters the trees in abstract beauty. The soul writhes in my beaked mouth, but I swallow it down whole.

The taste is magnificent. Spicy yet sweet at the same time. Like the best type of confection at Christmas. Stronger than gingerbread and more potent than rum cake. It infuses my whole being with warmth. Knowledge not my own floods my mind, and I am drunk off the sensation. The multitude of lives this soul has lived rushes through me. The gaping hole of need I have been feeling is now filled to the brim, and I don't know if I can take in any more. I have reached nirvana.

Very good, my child, the voice in my head echoes. *Now, complete your transformation.*

Pinfeathers push their way up and through my loose skin like fat needles. They angle every which way without beauty. The agony intensifies as fully formed feathers grow in next, black as ink and jagged. My vocal cords finally tear as I scream, blood collecting in the back of my throat. I am drowning. Then, I vomit the last things I consumed as a human. My hands and feet are knives as talons overtake my nails, wickedly curved. My beautiful blond hair falls out, and I am left transformed—an unnatural soul-eating abomination.

A sound pulls me out of my agony. The woman falls to the ground in shock and terror, the dead man prone before her in the unruly undergrowth. Her frosted air-rending screams are melodious and cause my skin to ripple in pleasure, newly formed feathers on my arms and neck rustle against one another, sticking up at odd angles. The clouds of mist coming from her mouth waft in the dancing breeze, not a care in the world. Like me.

The first light of dawn peeks over the hills. My red veiled world is blinded. I am no longer suited for the world of the day. I take one last look at the woman and vanish into smoke, descending into the depths of her nightmares as I flee the rays.

Until next the moon rises.

Sleep Walking

BARE FEET LEAVE TRAILS THROUGH the dust. Steps shamble down the forbidden hallway. The lock left broken in the moonlight. Ghosts of the past whisper, following the progress of her sleeping shuffle, seeing the strings dictating her movement emanating from the sealed room down the hall. The specters beg her to turn back. Plead with her to wake up. Somnambulist hands reach for the door. The one with paper and ink sealing the gaps. The air breathes as the religious brands break, ripped with the opening of the door, letting it out for the first time in a century.

Frozen Retribution

(Published in *Shiver: A Chilling Horror Anthology*, January 11, 2020)

FROST PATTERNS GREW IN FIDDLEHEAD spirals and snowflake fractals while suspended ice swirled at the command of Jack Frost. He was as old as the cold and as unforgiving as ice.

The winter sprite hung out on the roof of a skyscraper, watching the masses below. The humans, who could not see him, ignored or yelled at one another in a writhing mass of coats and hats. The humans' love of life and special spark had diminished to a bare flicker since the beginning of days. The poor souls needed to be reminded of what life could be.

Raising his hands, he let the snow fly downward onto the heads of the passersby in soft flakes that gathered on eyelashes. The adults just adjusted their bundles of layers and kept on. Not one looked up at the sky in wonder or excitement.

He flew on the wind to a nearby elementary school, where he dropped small heaps of fresh powder to make snow angels in, throw snowballs with, and, in general, just play around and enjoy. The bell for recess rang, and the children came out of the building, faces glued to their phones and video game devices. Not a single child played in his of-fering. It was only used to shove a small boy into face-first and then abandoned once the bell rang again.

Jack flew to an old folks' home, where he blew his frosted breath on the windows creating patterns and pictures to re-mind the occupants of simpler times and childhood mar-vels. All they did was complain about the cold and turn up the heaters in their rooms, melting away his offerings.

Done with humans, he isolated himself in a forest where the animals cowered from his chill or stalked their prey through his work, leaving deep footprints behind. Footprints Jack himself could never leave.

Ice blasted from Jack's hands. These people took their lives for granted. They did not notice the phenomena around them and only cared for themselves. In the past, stories had been told of the winter spirits and passed down to families who took care of each other. They respected their elders, not abandoning them to die in homes. They talked to one another face-to-face, forming memories together through experiences and daily physical interac-tions. If only Jack could have been born a human to ex-perience the joys and emotions they'd used to have in the olden days. To see life in its vibrancy and live through all the seasons.

Unfeeling ice exploded inside his heart, freezing it from the very core, murdering the last dregs of his ability to care for others.

A spring sprite flew by. Ice shard daggers flew from Jack's fingertips, clipping her wings.

"It's not your time yet. It's the season of death."

The poor fairy screamed in agony as she fell upon a spike of ice Jack had created in his anger a few minutes before. As she twitched, she faded from existence, no longer able to carry out the task she was created for.

"I will never see spring. I will never see its beauty or wonder. Neither will the humans. We will be the same."

January 12 started with a light snowfall over many of the northern states. The flakes were powdery and soft, blanketing the world into a white sea of wonder. Children stayed indoors to play video games online.

To change the tune of the humans, he allowed it to warm a bit, then summoned hail the size of fruit. Black ice formed from the melt off. The adults were furious about the damage. Cars with dented roofs and cracked windshields slid into collisions on all the major roads. Snowplows spun out, and the world shut down.

He plummeted the temperature again and stilled the wind. Hoarfrost grew like blacksmithed daggers. Photographers braved the frozen hellscape to capture the deadly beauty around them. Their praise was too little too late. Jack pulled them under drifts into hidden holes not to be found until spring.

By the seventeenth, everything was shut down, but it wasn't enough. He thickened the buildup on power lines and blew trees over with his frozen breath onto the wires. Power outages spread like the black plague. Heating systems were unable to fend off his assault. Hardly anyone in the cities had backup generators, and the elderly started dying from exposure in their own homes.

Jack cackled in delight. He had power over these mortals. He could not give them wonder but they could give him entertainment as they died.

Mother Nature sighed. Something had to be done. Her once kind-hearted frost spirit had turned on the people without her permission. There was no lesson being taught with the onslaught of cold and death. It was just for perverse pleasure.

With her long delicate fingers she created an adversary to put Mad Jack in his place. She molded and formed the perfect vessel. Now all she needed to do was make a bargain with Death.

It was the twenty-first, and Jack was doing his malicious business when something loomed in his peripherals. It was not large physically, but its presence was intense. A small girl with no visible wings was staring straight at him.

She couldn't be human, since she could see him, but she seemed like a normal kid. Getting closer he noticed her purple veins stood out against her clay skin. Her milky dead eyes met his own.

"Hello, Jack." Her voice was soft but carried on the wind. It was as terrible as cracking ice and just as hollow.

"Who are you?" he asked.

"I am Lucy. I speak for all of the humans you have killed the past few weeks." Her eyes did not blink.

"Interesting. Who sent you? What do you want?" Irritation crept into Jack's voice, turning it cold and flat.

"Mother Nature and Death. She created this clay body for me to inhabit while Death pulled me from my evaporation into nothingness, giving me a second life."

Jack thought she looked to be no older than seven. "Why you, though?"

Finally, she blinked. "I was the first human you killed on your rampage."

"That sucks. Well, Lucy, I'm off to spread more snow. See you later." Jack hopped onto a current to fly westward, only his ankle was caught.

"I must do my duty first, Jack, then you can be free." Her gray fingers wrapped all the way around his thin ankle.

Gathering his elemental magic into his palms he blasted her with the might of the arctic. Ice formed around her, encasing her, but she did not let go.

Death's scythe appeared and cracked her icy confines, coming to rest in her free hand.

She pulled Jack down to earth and stood on his feet, grounding him there.

"What are you—"

She touched her forehead to his. Memories of all the lives he had taken raked through his mind with dagger-like claws, ripping his conscience to shreds. Lights, colors, smells, and visions overlapped so quickly he blacked out from overstimulation.

He was a grandmother, cradling her sick grandchild in her freezing arms, both giving out their last visible breath at the same moment.

He was a father, driving desperately to find a doctor for his pregnant wife who was ill in bed, only to be hit by another car sliding on black ice. He died on impact. His wife gave birth at home, only to lose the child.

He was a little girl, toes gone and feet next, if only the infection had not spread faster than the gangrene.

With each memory torrenting through his mind his body got heavier and heavier. His heart was thawing. Lucy stepped off his feet but his legs felt like they were made of lead. He could not fly.

Falling to the ground, he cried tears of small ice grains. His heart felt bloated and full of sorrow, not only his pain but the dead's as well. As each new memory sliced through to the front of his mind, his memories of glee grew dark. There was no hope. No redemption for the damage he had caused needlessly.

Sure, he had caused blizzards before, but those had been at the request of Father Winter and Mother Nature. He had never gone out of his way to directly kill before. And now, each kill was a boulder on his back, crushing him without mercy.

"Lucy! Make it stop! Please!" Jack cried. "I won't do it again!"

Eerie eyes stared down at the distraught sprite. "I can't, Jack." The scythe glinted in the moonlight in her slack fingers.

"Kill me, then!"

Lucy took a step back, the bladed weapon disappearing from her grip. "No. Justice must be served."

In anguish, Jack threw himself down at her feet, the visions never ending. With a kill count of over six thousand and counting, he was consumed. Mother, father, sister, brother, son, daughter, infant, toddler. He was all of them, and yet their killer at the same time.

The cold began to seep into his hands and knees. The snow he was kneeling in felt freezing to him for the first time in his existence.

Looking down, he saw his hand beginning to fill out and turn the color of human flesh. He was turning into a human child. A human child alone in the tundra where he would die of exposure. He was finally getting his wish in the worst way possible.

Desperately, he looked around for Lucy, but she had vanished.

Cold seeped into his bones, his movements becoming sluggish. For the first time he could see his breath in the air, pluming in swirls of hazy clouds. In a way it was beautiful.

He tried to form an ice dagger to end it all. No magic jumped to his fingertips.

The onslaught of memories subsided as he lived out his own death. At first, he lost feeling in his extremities, then he stopped shivering. Hours ticked by. A fresh snowfall began to bury him alive. He could not move his arms or legs to drag himself out from his suffocating tomb. The sky was no longer visible. Darkness became his world.

He would not be found until spring.

Alice

ALICE TURNS HER HEAD, BLINKING into the darkness. A huge blanket is pulled up over her matted hair, covering her shiny eyes. She doesn't remember putting it there. Rhythmic breathing emanates from across the room. Her bedroom, the one she shares with Sally, the giantess who keeps her locked up in these four walls and now, hidden under cloth.

Alice reaches up, pulling the unicorn printed cover off her. It slithers to the ground with a muffled thump. Then she stands, gripping the wooden slats of the enormous chairback.

Sally wakes up, looks over at her moving doll, and screams.

Screaming Darkness

(Published in *Beneath* by Ghost Orchid Press, May 5, 2021)

DISINTERRED DUST BILLOWS AROUND MY sneakers. The Paris catacombs confine me, squeezing me onward through its narrow tunnels. Hallways of water fill my shoes. The graffiti stopped miles back.

Something screams behind me.

I whip around, my hair raising at the dark emptiness lined in looming shadowy bones.

Jogging, I try to remember the directions to the nearest manhole exit to the surface. My phone died hours ago, so I'm going on memory. The flashlight flickers. A shriek sounds directly behind my right ear, something swiping at my blistered feet. I drop the flashlight and sprint. Screaming darkness consumes me.

The Lochs of Brough

MEGAN KNEW SHE WAS DONE for. Callum and Rachel had tied her up and stuffed her in their car's trunk. The zip ties on her wrists cut into her, letting a trickle of blood slick her skin. Twisting and pulling, she only succeeded in cutting deeper.

Bump. Bump. Bump.

The backroads of Scotland weren't paved, causing her to jostle and actually hit the top of the lid of the trunk at times, causing her ears to ring and shoulders to jam in their sockets. Left alone to her thoughts, she seethed. Sure, she had lured Callum's little brother for that man to kidnap, but she had been threatened! It was self-defense the jury had said. His life for hers. Not enough justice for Callum and his girlfriend, apparently. Vigilantes, the both of them.

She rattled around for an eternity before the car finally parked.

"Get her out." Callum's ire was audible even from inside the trunk.

The impatient turn of a key sounded like a death knell. She was so dead.

Scattered sunlight blinded Megan as she finally got to breathe in fresh air again. It had been hours rebreathing her own exhales in that godforsaken trunk.

"Leave me alone!" she screamed.

Callum just laughed in her face. "Like you did to my brother? Did he beg you to help him escape? We're giving you an even better chance than you gave him. Be grateful." He reached in and roughly hauled her out of the trunk onto the rocky dirt road. "No one will hear you scream, but no one will be holding you hostage, either."

Rachel reached down and cut the zip ties binding Megan's ankles and wrists while Callum held her down by the hips and head.

"People say this place is haunted," taunted Rachel. "Pray you make it back to civilization when you wake up."

A tire iron to the back of the head, and Megan was out.

Slowly, her consciousness surfaced. Something cold numbed her face; hard-packed dirt from the smell. She cracked her eyes open. It took a while for things to come into focus, but at last she took in her surroundings. They'd left her alone at the ruins of an abandoned castle in northern Scotland. Without her phone and pocket wifi.

The moon peeked through the large trees encroaching on the fallen stones of the once modest castle. The upper floors were gone, and all that seemed accessible now was the basement.

Megan got up, head splitting in pain from the movement. Clouds rolled in abnormally fast, releasing their rain on the landscape.

A screech turned Megan's blood to ice. Images of death flashed before her eyes before the elongated scream subsided. It came from the waterfall that fell into the nearby loch. Was this place actually haunted? She didn't believe in the supernatural, but if a banshee did exist, that was what they'd sound like.

The rain picked up into a downpour. The short leather jacket she wore was not enough to protect her from the elements. Her pants and shoes were soaked, toes already pruning. Better to venture down into the basement chambers to explore until the downpour stopped. Afterward, she would hike to the nearest town and get help. Then she would press charges for kidnapping and attempted murder.

Picking her way through the rubble, she found the uncovered entrance to the lower levels. Water rushed down the stone steps ahead of her. Gingerly, she made her way down into the bowels. There was no light to see by, so she had to make do with touch and echoes.

The stone foundations were rough and damp beneath her fingers, interspersed with slick moss. She walked in a few yards to get past the rain whipping through the opening.

Once she was able to find something hard to sit on, she settled in for the night.

Her head pounded from that damned crowbar. It felt so good to be sitting again. Just rest for a bit. Her eyelids grew heavy despite her attempts to keep a lookout.

A growl echoed from the labyrinth of chambers she could not see into, snapping her out of her sleep. Was there a wild animal in here? Or another person?

"Hello?" she called.

A scraping sound filled her ears. Something was rubbing against the stone, approaching her. She backtracked to the wet entrance where there would be light to see by. Squinting, she could see small flickers of light outlining a creature. Each step was a distinct *clunk*.

Slowly, step by wobbly step, a small man emerged from the inky darkness, his white hair long and scraggly under his red hat. His flint-like fingers trailed alongside him against the stone walls, leaving sparks in their wake. His shoes were made of iron.

Screaming at the sight, Megan ran up the steps, but his long strong fingers grabbed one of her sore ankles, pulling her back down into the darkness. All the air fled her lungs as she smashed against the floor.

"You will help make the foundations stronger," whispered the creature, its voice cracked and gravelly as if it had not spoken for a century.

Heaving strangled gulps of air, Megan kicked out at the small man, her foot stopping a millimeter before his face. His iron grip had caught and crushed her ankle in his small hand, her bone shards grinding against each other. She screamed once again, noticing too late that he had grabbed hold of her other ankle as well.

Crunch. Pure agony.

"Come, girly, I have a special place just for ye." His fingers pulled Megan by her ankles, his weighted shoes not allowing her to gain any leverage to pull him with her toward the entrance, toward freedom.

Twisting was her only course of action available, sending blades of fire through her throbbing legs. Futile.

Upon reaching the end of a corridor, the fay let go of her with one spindly hand but immediately bent her knees forward.

Snap, pop. Snap, pop. Both were now folding the wrong direction.

"I need ye tae fit. No use screamin' 'bout it," he commented as she grabbed her face so hard her nails drew bloody gashes down her pale cheeks.

While she sobbed, he pulled a thin layer of stone out of the way to reveal a hidden crawl space big enough for a contortionist.

"In here. We need these foundations to be strong with sacrifices, an' you'll do nicely."

He started shoving her into the confined space, centipedes and spiders trying to escape around her, abandoning their ancient home. She could not see them in the darkness, only feel their many legs and writhing bodies. Some were squishier than others, crushed beneath her face while others wriggled down her shirt and across her arms with thousands of synchronized limbs. With her legs spiraled in on themselves, she could almost fit. He kept pushing, but her head was against the damp moss-covered stone in the claustrophobic space. Something was crawling over her ear she could not dislodge.

I'm going to die, and no one will find me, she thought.

"Wait here. I'll be back," the small man said.

Her chance! Determination filled Megan's overwrought mind. She must survive. She'd even apologize to Rachel and Callum.

Scooting out inch by excruciating inch, head last, she managed to escape the sarcophagus and finally remove the beetle crawling into her ear and the last centipede from down her shirt. Unrolling her legs made her black out for a moment, their pops and cracks sickening and tendons useless.

Dragging the lower half of her body, she turned a corner in the pitch darkness, and then another, still not seeing the glimmer of moonlight. Finally, she turned a third. Light! Freedom was hers!

Slice.

Why was she looking up at her own torso?

Something was in her hair, lifting her up. "You will fit now, young lass."

She was eye level with the small creature brandishing a bloody scythe. She was no longer connected to her body.

Shadows

Gentle fingers caress your hair. Sweet words fall from invisible lips. Your friend. They say they're not human but from a distant place of wonder. You believe them when they command the shadows. Twisting darkness forming shapes, prancing about the room like a circus act. You giggle in delight at the magical show. Until the dark animals converge, staring you down. Then they jump down your throat.

Twin

HER RANCID BREATH CARESSED THE shell of my ear as I lay under the stifling covers. I dared not come up for air, in fear it would break the connection. My other half, my heart, was back. She was no longer lying in the grave, but next to me, under the blankets, my own tomb, where the gaze of the moon could not touch her. She was a rotting corpse who loved me beyond death. Fingers carded through my hair, leaving the prickling of needles in their wake along my scalp.

"I've come to take you with me," she whispered.

Fairy Godmother
(Published in *Frost Zone Zine*, March 7, 2022)

ANGELA.

The word tickled my mind when I was almost asleep, giving me goosebumps even though I was buried under thick blankets and a huge pile of teddy bears hugging me goodnight. She was here again.

Tell me what you wish for . . . I can grant it. For a small price of course.

She was doing it again, asking me to wish for something. Mom always said I needed to work for what I wanted. Rainbow Teddy was for pulling weeds for a week. I ignored her.

Invisible boney fingers longer than a human's lightly touched my shoulder as I fell asleep. *Dream about it, my sweet.*

She started singing about children and crunchy bones.

Nibbles died. My tears fell to her fluffy white body, soaking into her fur as I clutched her to my chest, running to show Mom.

"She was an old rabbit, sweetie. We'll bury her tonight when Dad gets home."

"How do I fix her?" I pleaded.

"Oh honey, there's nothing you can do. Sometimes there are things you can't fix no matter how much you try." She reached down to take Nibbles away, but I ran to my room, hugging my first friend.

"I'll make my first wish!" I called out.

Very good. What is it you wish for my pet?

The woman's deep voice in my mind gave me goosebumps again. I could feel her fingers in my hair as she walked around me.

"Fix Nibbles," I whimpered.

As you wish.

She became visible, her hand rushing toward the side of my head. Something was inside my ear, tingling. *Twist, crack, splinter.* Knives stabbed me deep inside. I heard the snap at the same time as my scream. Black spots filled my vision, and I fell to the floor.

"Angela!" Mom ran through the open doorway, not seeing the tall dark lady with wings.

The fairy godmother chuckled.

I saw what looked like a small string of three tiny bones in the creature's hands, broken and white, ripped from inside my ear. She popped them into her mouth and began to crunch.

I looked down at Nibbles, still in my arms. She was moving, her eyes bright. Her long white ears lay flat against her head as she began to struggle, long feet flailing.

Resurrection has a high price, my dear. The words echoed through my head.

Six months later, the sunbeams on the funeral held in the backyard shone through the X-ray I was holding. I could see where the missing bones from my left ear I could no longer hear out of should be. My missing pieces. There was a shadow of fairy wings over the dark picture, and any other picture taken of me now.

"Do you wish to say a few words over Nibbles?" Mom asked.

I couldn't cry for Nibbles again. I shook my head, my heart frozen. Regret hit me as vertigo, my new friend, showed up again. Ground became sky as I hit the grass. I had gotten Nibbles for only a few more months. Not worth it. I would never wish again.

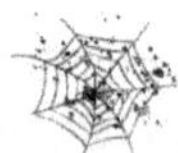

"We have to get rid of most of our stuff so we can move to the new apartment," Mom explained. "There won't be as much room there. You can only take one of your old stuffed animals."

Would that lady fairy creature be left behind with the empty home? With excitement I dumped all my teddy bears, unicorns, and dragons into a donation bag except Rainbow Teddy. We were moving away from the mistake I had made three years ago.

We got situated in the van and drove to the new apartment complex. It was on the other side of town, twenty minutes away. But would it be far enough?

I sat Rainbow Teddy on my new twin-size bed with a

blue comforter and pulled out the Polaroid camera I had gotten for my birthday. My lungs squeezed tight as the camera slipped in my clammy grip. Would she be there? Was I free?

Flash. The small picture slowly emerged from the base of the camera. I took it and held it with two fingers, waiting for it to develop.

Darkness.

Faint shapes.

I shook it to air it out more, make it develop faster. My slick fingers fumbled. The photo hit the floor. My heart dropped with it.

It was facedown, picture side on the carpet.

Gingerly, I bent to pick up my hope of a more normal life. My head tilted forward, and my world flipped and spun. I froze in place, gripping the side of my bed, trying not to throw up from the vertigo. Why was I moving my head again? What was worth this?

Freedom.

Once the room righted itself and I could swallow again, I grasped the closest corner of the small Polaroid and flipped it. There she was, a haze with glinting teeth that crunched bones like candy, wide dragonfly-like wings spread out behind her. She had followed. I would never be able to escape. There was nothing I could do. I would pay almost anything to get rid of this fairy phantom so I could have my life to myself for the first time since her original nighttime whisper. No more inquiries about what I wanted and promises to fulfill every dream I could have with the price of bone. No more long invisible fingers caressing me in my sleep while dark lullabies echoed in my mind.

You can't escape me, my pet.

"I wish you would leave me alone and never come back."
Crunch.

Demon of Spring

THE SKIN PEELS FROM THEIR back in four large strips. A breeze makes them flutter like the wings they are morphing into. Another head with huge faceted eyes comes through the human mouth, the human grin splitting to accommodate. The skull is now a decoration of death upon the thorax. Appendages slough off extra human flesh, revealing thin black legs where the skeleton should be. The tailbone elongates and straightens, piercing through the skin, a sharpened stinger. Buzzing fills the air as the wings take flight. A demon of spring released.

Deadline

DARRYL SLID A DOLLAR IN quarters into the vending machine and weighed his options. The resounding thuds of the coins inside the appliance was familiar. The pretzels looked inviting, but so did the cookies. The smell of coffee wafted from the nearby kitchen where his coworkers were on break, working late into the night. They were on deadline again.

Thoughts seeped through his porous mind, melted from long hours staring at the screen. The film was due tomorrow. This was the last night of overtime for this particular project. The director had once again given last-minute notes that could have been addressed months ago, but no, he hadn't been able to make up his mind, and here Darryl was.

Thunk. The pretzels landed in the bottom of the machine he worshiped. Grabbing them, he turned to go back to his desk. Six more hours until the turnover of the last CG work to the color grader. Six more hours until he could see Carol-Anne and their son Timothy. Hug them, and then crawl into bed for a week. Then take a vacation to catch up with Tim, who had started baseball while Darryl had been too busy working. The next project was already starting to ramp up. He could dream, anyway.

To get back to his desk, Darryl had to pass the creature stand-in statue that had been lent from the set. A horror film, of course, like most of the films the studio worked on. The hairs on the back of his neck rose from slumber to stand on end as he approached the draped larger-than-life figure.

Normally, during the daylight hours, this particular set piece did not bother him, but tonight, from the depths of the hood, eyes seemed to actually appear. No longer was it the mannequin head of smooth styrene, with no eyes carved into its dark painted surface. There was definitely something watching him from under the robe.

Darryl's feet shuffled along the industrial carpet, watching the glow of amber, usually applied only in the computer, follow him from under the costume hood.

Three feet.

Two feet.

One foot.

He was now side by side with it. A faint puff of air caressed his sensitive neck. The creature breathing.

In terror, Darryl broke company policy and handled the set prop, yanking the starched fireproof hood back to reveal the monstrosity underneath.

Smooth black-painted styrene looked back at him. No amber to be seen.

Why aren't you working, Darryl? The words echoed in his mind.

Startled, Darryl looked around and only saw people staring at their monitors in the dark, working at a fever pitch. None spared him a look or even seemed to have noticed him breaking protocol.

You won't be able to afford those pretzels if you don't continue bringing me to life.

He froze mid step. "What?"

That got the closest coworker's attention. She pulled her headphones down. "What did you say, Darryl? Is the animation broken for your shot?" She looked at him quizzically. "I can do a re-export if you need it."

"Oh. No thanks, Amber. Everything's fine." He shook his head to clear it. "Just talking to myself, I guess."

"Okay." She sank back into her ergonomic chair and headphones, oblivious to the voice that was now chuckling in Darryl's head.

I wanted to personally thank you for giving me life, Darryl. Without your expertise they would have never got my glowing eyes right to see into my soul, releasing it into this domain.

A tremor ran through his whole body as ice shot through his veins. *What are you talking about?* he thought back.

I watched as you developed the technique to bring me to life. Sold your soul for it, even.

I didn't sell my soul for anything! he yelled back in his head.

"Are you okay, Darryl?" Lucy had exited the kitchen. The comforting smell of mocha washed over Darryl as she approached. "You look pale. Only six more hours, bud.

You've got this. We're so close being done. Going home."

"Yeah. Can't wait to go home." He staggered to his own desk and fell into his well-worn chair, wiggling the mouse on reflex to bring the monitor to life. Like the main monster now in his head.

I didn't sell my soul, he insisted.

Oh Darryl. When was the last time you ate dinner with your family? Your family was so important to you. Your soul, you could say. You gave them up to give me life. Such long hours to provide them a home and food. You loved them by letting them go. You loved them by creating me. The feel of long, invisible nails ran down Darryl's back before coming up to rest in his hair, anointing him. *All you have left to do is complete the final three shots, and I'll be given new life on the screen, entering millions of nightmares the world over, fueling my corporeal body with long life and the powers of darkness.*

Invisible strings attached themselves to his wrists, placing his hands at the mouse and keyboard, into the familiar grooves he had worn into them over the years.

Click. He watched as his hands moved on muscle memory, pulling up the compositing script to place the glowing eyes of the monster in his mind into the frames of the last shots of the film.

I don't want to do this. The words echoed in his occupied mind. *The world already has so many monsters. Why would I want to release you to the world in reality?*

If you don't, you'll be fired. How will you support your family? You'll lose your house. Your reputation in the industry will be ruined. You'll have to start over in a new field you're not qualified for. The nails in his hair dug into his scalp, pulling on unwashed locks. *Is it worth losing your family this way as well?*

Darryl felt some of the tension loosen from his body. *I can't lose this job. What are a few more nightmares going to do to the world?* He clicked on the gizmo to create the shape of the eyes and track them to the actor that had been in the costume on display in the studio now.

Thank you, Darryl.

His hands moved automatically, color picking the glow and adjusting the intensity to match the values of the eyes in the rest of the movie. The intensity of the flames of brimstone reflected back in his glasses as he gazed deep into the CG eyes to make sure they captured the soul of the demon.

He pressed play to watch the eyes and make sure they lined up where they should be for the whole shot. A few tweaks later and they seemed to take on a life of their own. The shot was of the monster gloating over a family man whom he had defeated.

You understand me so well, Darryl. You capture my soul and bring it into the visual spectrum where I've never dwelt. I've been trapped in the red-marked pages of the script where they kept changing my innards, deciding what made me tick. It was so uncomfortable, Darryl. Do you know what it feels like to have your mind, your inner workings, toyed with because they weren't feeling it that day?

Yes, Darryl thought. *I pour my heart and soul into this work, and they tell me to go a different direction. A direction I don't understand. One that'll be more profitable but weakens the story. Weakens my art.*

You can be proud of me, dear Darryl. I will be your masterpiece.

He submitted the shot to dailies to be reviewed and approved. The supervisors were on the clocks as much as the artists these days. Approval should come in minutes.

Ding! Darryl opened the note: *Approved, move onto the next one.*

He closed out the file and opened the next one. *So what are you going to do once you're all the way in our world?* His hands moved in nearly automated accuracy. Roto out the eyes, glow, color, add soul. In this shot he only needed to add the eye treatment to the first little bit of the shot before CG swirls of ethereal darkness took over the frame as the monster entered into the family man on the floor, taking over his body.

Well, revenge on that one script writer who tried to kill me at the end of the film would be a beautiful form of justice.

The fingers dug a little deeper into his scalp as if trying to massage his brain through his skull.

Darryl tried to ignore it as the images rendered and he sent them to dailies.

Ding! Approved. Next.

The final shot of the film. The dreaded ending where the family man opens his eyes to reveal the glow of the monster that has taken over. The classic "poor bastard becomes the devil" ending.

Darryl's fingers paused. *Will you be taking over my body or will you have your own?*

I will take over your own and don that cloak on the mannequin, corporeal at last.

A dark chuckle rang through Darryl's mind, echoing with promise. His blood turned to frozen nitrogen in his veins, ethereal transformation already taking a hold. His eyes faintly took on the glow of the monster's, reflecting off the color correct monitor. *You're already taking over me, aren't you?*

Yes, my dark liberator.

Panic welled up Darryl, his insides squirming with dread, the pretzels now sitting like rocks. *I'll never be able to see my family again if I become you. I won't put them in that kind of danger!*

When do you ever see them, anyway? They won't miss you any more than they already do. You only use your body to do the bidding of others, anyway. This won't be much of a change for you, except for the powers you will gain. Break the unending cycle of moving from project to project, bowing to the creative control of others, no end in sight.

The idea was so tempting. To be in control of his own life. He dragged the roto tool over the actor's eyes. But what about his family? He wouldn't be able to support them if he lost this job. He was almost fifty years old. Too late to change careers if he tarnished his name and didn't finish this movie.

Will my family be safe if I do this? he thought to the monster.

From us, yes.

He had to do it. He had to finish this task. *I need to make sure they'll be supported. It needs to look like I died so they can get the insurance money. Carol-Anne will be able to move on then.*

Fine by me.

Okay. I'll do it. His fingers flew over the keyboard shortcuts as he did the color corrections, glow, and fine tuning to reflect the flames of hell. Flames that would soon be engulfing him. The final images rendered perfectly, a miracle. Or was it an omen?

He submitted the final shot of his final film. His masterpiece.

Wait—

Ding! Final shot approved.

The long, bony fingers in his hair dissolved. Darryl watched the reflection in the monitor as the creature of darkness fully took over his body. His bones lengthened, cracking before filling in with new, nonhuman marrow. His skin darkened to living shadows, like the black body paint the actor had worn, augmented by twisting tendrils of darkness. The dark cloak lifted off the mannequin and settled over his new visage. Through it all, his eyes glowed with the fires of damnation.

Cloak of Bones

THE MOONLIGHT REFLECTED SHARPLY OFF the silver buckles and dark vials in the bandolier slung low over the man's torso, peeking through the parting of his midnight cloak. Tools of the trade.

As he entered the cemetery, the dead who yearned to be reborn scratched at their confining coffins. They still had living families to be reunited with. Through the pristine rows of graves he roamed, going further back in time the farther he walked. The fog thickened and crystalized in his presence, obscuring the long-forgotten names carved in eternal stone.

Feral cats cowered from his advance and crickets stilled, abandoning their hymns. Ghostly apparitions fled in fear of being given life again by one who scoffed at celestial law and broke every taboo with malice. Grass died beneath his feet, leaving withered footprints in his wake. An oozing chill emanated from his very being, the by-product of being frozen in time.

On the other side of the Christian fence, he spied the

perfect target. Phasing through the barrier, he lazily stroked the tombstone with a long pale finger. The neglected common rock of two hundred years was cracked with rampant poisonous overgrowth twisting in on itself, strangling, marking it unclean. Etched into it was the word "Witch," along with her death date 114 years ago.

With a whistle, he summoned his former project. A squat figure approached; the putrid smell of maggot-ridden meat bound together only by ethereal strings of dark magic preceded them. They never said a word but bowed low just outside arm's reach of the tall thin man.

"Dig," the necromancer commanded, his voice smooth and uncaring.

Dirt flung up in embankments, moist earth heady, overpowering the short man's stench. The moon hid from the sight of desecration, its pure light not able to witness the works of darkness.

Crack! The shovel hit wood. With methodical precision from far too many years of practice, the creature widened the hole and crafted steps for his creator, resurrector. Then, with the might of a brute, he tore the exposed coffin lid from its rightful place and threw it out of the way. Desperately, he scrambled to extricate himself from the earthy tomb and bowed to the man in shadow.

"There is a small mass grave two yards east. Dig there next," the man commanded.

Cloak open wide, the master of the shadow arts descended into the freshly excavated site. She was beautiful. Pure bones cleaned by the writhing insects still searching for their next meal.

The man extracted a vial from his belt containing a substance of the deepest violet, flecked with pewter. He anointed the broken crown of the skull and began to chant memorized passages from a sacred text long forgotten by the world.

The jawbone twitched and jabbered. A voice from the dust screamed through it, ringing through the air like a death knell. "Gabriel!"

"Evening, Lilith. I never thought I'd find you in this country."

"No. You should be dead. Why haven't you aged?" she whispered through her long bleached teeth. "It took me fifty years to be free of you in life. What more could you possibly want?"

"There's a little boy I need, but the wards melt flesh. I need you to bring him to me."

"What boy? Whose child?" Her maternal instincts could not be quelled despite her own children being long dead, two at his own hand.

Gabriel adjusted his perfectly poised hood, pulled out a dagger, and sliced his palm, dripping the lifeblood onto the remains of the corpse. "You are bound to me, to my will, my word, and my life. You will not question or hesitate to follow orders." A glow emanated from the picked clean bones. Hatred poured off Lilith as her will was sealed away, reduced to a pawn.

Gabriel chanted, drawing runes in the air with his wand-like finger. The bones twitched as gnarled roots twisted and bound them, forming a moveable host for her resurrected consciousness. The creaking and groaning of plant and calcium filled the empty cemetery as Lilith rose from the grave. Insects fell like a shed shroud and freshly dug earth plummeted into the deserted coffin. A wail reverberated through the air, hollow and undead.

She was bound to the man she hated most. There was no country to flee to this time, no new identity to hide behind. No escape.

"You'll need a cloak to perform this task, one of my own design," he said. He gave her a lazy sidelong look. "Unbaptized infant bones."

Lilith stilled, seeming to want to protest the use of such unfortunate remains but unable to voice her complaint.

Stepping down into the mass grave freshly excavated, Gabriel pulled a small bell from its pouch in the bandolier.

Lilith buried her face of bone in her hands.

His spindle fingers rang it once. Its peal continued echoing through the empty skulls, morphing into the cackles of demons. The earth was rent in twain, the fires of hell bellowing thick, charcoal hued smoke and misery into the air. Unholy spawn crawled from the flames of damnation, slithering into the skulls of the infants, illuminating the eye sockets in a red blaze. The metallic heat of brimstone was familiar grit in Lilith's teeth, echoing of her past.

Another chant, and the bones along with the eerie skulls were woven with the thin roots of a weeping willow into a cloak. It would give the gift of shadow walking between the planes: into one shadow and out another in the blink of an eye.

"You will find the boy I want you to retrieve in Dormer Manor, up the river about ten miles. It's the only manor with active wards around it. You'll know it when their frequencies reverberate through your teeth." Gabriel put his long fingers into a pocket and drew out a Y-shaped rod. "I have acquired a drop of his blood and applied it to the tip of this divining rod. It will point you to him."

Lilith tentatively took the small metal rod in her skeletal hands, the protruding end sticking forward yet wanting to turn north.

"You are not to sabotage the divining rod in anyway. The blood stays on, even after the boy is found," he commanded.

She nodded and placed it into the fist of an infant arm inside the cloak. Its tiny fingers gripped it tightly.

"Off you go, then. I'll be waiting here, working."

With as much of a sneer as she could convey without lips, Lilith took off through the shadows toward the river. The darkness between entering one shadow and teleporting to the next was like swimming through black oil. It slicked between her ribs and down her vertebrae. She had no lungs to breathe with but mentally held her breath all the same.

The babbling of the river was soothing and lulled her into a rhythm. Enter one shadow cast by the full moon, exit another, sound with the divining rod. After a few miles of repetition, the rod began to move eastward, away from the river.

The manor house loomed tall in a clearing. Invisible tendrils and shields swarmed and buzzed around the home, but her witchy consciousness with decades of practice could see them. Tendrils snapped out at her, threatening to dispatch her if she came any closer. Their dark purplish-black hue sang of the malevolent nature of their spellwork. This would need some careful study and work.

With no tools of her trade to aid her except the divining rod and demonic cloak of bones, she would be hard-pressed to do this undetected in one night. Perhaps she could use one of her own bones as a wand? Looking around her for tools in the surrounding woods, she saw a sharp glint of obsidian on the ground.

The dark shard could draw blood if drawn against flesh. It would do perfectly to carve runes into herself and transform her very limbs into wands. Runes of protection along her ribs would help in her endeavor as well.

Roots creaked as she bent, testing the limits of her flexibility in organic bindings. She could bend completely in half both forward and backward with her loose hips and no restricting tendons or bulky muscles to get in the way.

Raising the black stone to her left hand, she contemplated what ancient ruins would best suit her needs and not interfere with the necromancy magic keeping her alive and bound. Perhaps some basic cuneiform?

Without muscle memory to hinder her, she seemed to be ambidextrous. After carving the needed runes to channel her magic on her left, accounting for the human bone's energies, she moved onto her right hand and arm. The rectangular shapes of the writing system crossed one another in complex patterns starting at the tip of her index finger, down to her palm, wrist, elbow, collarbones, and across her ribs over to where her heart had once been; the center of her magical being. Both arms could now channel her darker magics and funnel them to the tips of her index fingers. She would expand it to all of her fingers eventually if needed, but this would be a start.

Stowing the obsidian in a tiny baby hand, she looked to the partially veiled stars; half the night gone. Time to enter the house.

Lilith took a step toward the back door. Instantly a shielding bubble surrounding the home enlarged, expanding toward her location, sensing her evil intent. The intent thrust upon her. Unfazed, she continued forward, letting the dark purple envelope her. It oozed around her bones seeking flesh to melt, to no avail. She had passed the first obstacle.

Oozing, ethereal tendrils of green snapped out at her, this time healing wards. They slid over her, searching for her blood to recognize if she was one to protect, one keyed in as to be saved using house magics. Her marrow tingled in recognition, but to no avail. She was past healing in this state. Why would her blood be keyed into this random estate's wards? Were they just looking for magical signatures in the bloodlines?

Silvery webs now materialized along the stone and brickwork, shrouding the house, their strands glittering with power. Lilith raised an etched finger, tracing out a rune pattern to help her analyze this new barrier. A ward of good luck and receiving one's heart's desires. A shiver of nostalgia passed through her as her magic came into contact with it. She had woven similar barriers in her lifetime. It would have an anchor point somewhere on the grounds, or in a cornerstone of the home. She would need to undo this one if she were to be successful in her quest.

Lilith walked to the cornerstone that seemed to be pulsing with the most power. The northeast. Crouching down, the bony tip of her finger caressed a sigil she had never seen before. Quite ingenious in its array. She would have to scry for its counter sign.

As she reached for the obsidian shard in her cloak, the baying of animals sounded around the side of the estate. Their barks were deep and wet, unrecognizable.

Reluctantly, Lilith ripped her consciousness in two, sending one side to sink into the depths of her mind to focus on scrying the counter in the glinting obsidian. The remaining part screamed in agony at the forced split, retaining only enough of itself to fight on animal instinct with gnashing teeth and whipping magic, and to hold the obsidian still in front of her left eye.

The hounds rounded the corner, bearing down on her, fangs snapping at where her appendages and neck had been. There were four of them, as tall as she was and as well built as grizzlies. Eyes glowed red with the intent to rend and protect. Like her, they were undead. Reanimated to withstand.

Her fingers sliced the air, leaving binding chains in their wake, flying toward the closest beast, twisting around it like boa constrictors and biting like vipers. The monster howled in rage but stayed down.

Snap! More teeth closed in around the space her throat had just vacated.

Lilith used her cloak to slink into one hound's shadow and emerge out another's, all while holding the obsidian steady. The deeper consciousness was whispering intently as vague shapes were appearing in the black reflections.

Bam! The hound she had snuck up on through the shadows kicked backward at her, sending her flying. Her ribcage held, thanks to the cuneiform, but creaked and groaned on impact.

There! The counter sign!

The remaining three beasts pounced on her at once. She threw the cloak over herself and sank into the shadows of the tree she had been kicked into.

The unbaptized infant skulls glowed around her as she stayed in the space between. Glowed enough for her to memorize the counter sign by. It was all sharp edges, opposite the curling elegance of the ward sigil.

Lilith tried to combine her two consciousnesses again, but they were like oil on water now. She'd take care of that after destroying the beasts.

She emerged from the shadow of the house, roundhouse kicking a hound in the snout, pushing the calm half of her consciousness into the beast. It ran along its nervous system to the brain, analyzing where the anchor point was. The nape of the neck.

Lilith took the obsidian shard in a clenched fist, jumped, and drove it into the back of the second beast's neck, between vertebrae, severing the magical reanimating strings from their anchor. She called her consciousness back into herself. The beast fell, immediately decaying beyond usability.

Crunch! Her neck ground between the fangs of the third hound, shards splintering. Willow roots slithered around the vertebrae to keep them together. Lilith drove her fingers straight into the open eyes of the beast, plunging straight through to the brain and wiggled them, scrambling everything she could reach inside the cranium.

The beast jerked, releasing her momentarily. It was enough. She swung onto its back and plunged the obsidian into the nape. One left.

She sank once more into the shadows and re-emerged under the last beast's head. It reared back, trying to get in biting range, but it was too late. She clambered up its shoulder and plunged the shard home one last time.

If she'd had lungs, she was sure she would be breathing hard. And feel sad for the demise of the poor creatures only doing what they were created for. However, she didn't want to die again yet. She would figure out how to break her binding and kill the unkillable necromancer.

Crouching down at the scrawling sigil, she etched her own on top, negating the final ward. The sound of a bone cracking deep within the stone resonated through her. The ward had been made with a sacrifice of one of the warder's own bones. Someone really wanted this place protected.

Time to slip inside and retrieve the boy.

The hallways were bright and beautiful, murals covering every wall, entwining sigils and family history together. No time to analyze. Gabriel was waiting.

She took out the divining rod with the boy's blood and continued on, slipping from shadow to shadow to an inner room.

There he was. A young boy of about six, sleeping with long black hair haloing his head on a down pillow. He'd slept through the whole ordeal outside. Peaceful. Like all children should be. Like she wished her own children had been.

Her desire to protect this child with her whole soul erupted in her chest, making her see red, her consciousnesses boiling together once again with a united purpose. She just had to—

The binding engulfed her once again, whipping the thought from her mind. What was she doing again? Taking this sacrifice to Gabriel.

Tenderly, she twirled her fingers over the boy, deepening his dreams. She scooped him up and held him close under the cloak. Together they melted into a shadow

And re-emerged back in the graveyard.

Lilith placed the boy at the necromancer's feet. There

was nothing she could do to save his skin, and any connection to him would just hurt her emotional scars.

Gabriel took the sleeping boy and tossed him on the low altar he had constructed out of broken tombstones he had pilfered.

"Time to waken the boy. We want him to be able to experience this honor, after all." The ring of a bell from his bandolier later, and the boy's eyes blinked open.

"What's going on? Who are you? Where's Dad?"

Gabriel chuckled. "Now, now, Draven. Don't you worry. Your precious daddy will join you soon. On the other side, that is."

Draven struggled against the binds, his head whipping to either side as the newly procured ropes bit into his wrists.

Lilith seethed though her porcelain teeth yet stayed out of the ritual circle. She would not be brought into one again by this man. She had done her time already.

"Come here, Lilith," Gabriel commanded. "Hold him down while I execute the ritual."

Against her will, her feet began dragging forward toward the altar. She could not stop them. His command over her was gaining strength. His blood magic was strong.

With each step, the eyes of the child bore into her hollow sockets. A storm of guilt warred in her. What could she do? She was not powerful enough. She didn't even have enough of her own blood to try and counteract Gabriel's.

"I sacrifice you, Draven Livingston . . ."

If Lilith had still had a beating heart, it would have faltered. Livingston. He was sacrificing one of her own progenies. Blood of her blood. Bone of her bone. He was stealing from her yet again. And she had helped.

Despair crashed over her, drowning out her hearing. Was there nothing she could do to escape this man? He had taken Thomas and Draxton from her already, robbing them of their life, and now one of the descendants of her baby Nathaniel. Was she truly cursed to always lose those she loved to an early death at the hand of this devil? A devil she had spilled blood for. Her own blood. And now, even more blood of her blood.

Blood of her blood. The idea rang in her hollow skull. She could use his blood to power her own blood magic and overturn Gabriel.

She screamed as she split her mind in two once more, trying with all her willpower to contain the part with the binding to Gabriel to the back of her skull in one of the mental boxes she usually kept information in to pull up for later uses. The bond ravaged her memories with deep claws as it was dragged backward and temporarily sealed.

Stealthily, she touched the drop of blood on the divining rod to begin her own ritual. Words echoed in her skull, words of power, killing intent, and love. The mental box rattled dangerously. She chanted faster.

Gabriel lifted the dagger high, chanting his own ritual to elongate his miserable existence.

Lilith removed the cloak of bones from her shoulders and swept it over Draven, plunging him into the shadow realm. Out of reach for now.

The knife sunk into the tombstone, cracking it in half.

Gabriel screamed in rage. "How dare you defy your binding! You are mine! Always have been, always will be."

"Not anymore," she gritted out. Her hands shot out, fingers jabbing through Gabriel's chest, into his heart. She crooked her fingers, widening the punctured holes, feeling the frozen blood within.

Gabriel laughed. "You think you can kill me with a flesh wound? I, who command the dead?"

Lilith released her magic and mind fragment, slamming it into the ventricles of his heart. As her magic drained into him, the part of her mind with the binding broke free, destroying the knowledge that had been in the box with it.

"What have you done to me?" Gabriel whispered as liquid red began to pulse from his chest wounds.

"I gave you a mother's love. It's enough to thaw any heart." Her arms retracted from Gabriel, as they now no longer were permitted to harm him. "You feel for Draven as if he were your own flesh and blood. If you survive, you will save him from the shadow realm, and never harm him nor his loved ones." She could feel her unbound consciousness fading as it melded with Gabriel's. "You will never hurt my family again."

The moon shone down upon Lilith as she fell to her knees, the ghostly apparitions of the cemetery's departed looking on from afar. All she had left now was her weaker, bound fragment of a mind. A tear of morning dew slipped down her unfeeling skull. At least her legacy was secured by her love.

TWISTED PSYCHOLOGY

Pep Pill

FEELING DOWN? TAKE A PEP Pill! Increase your dopamine, lose weight, sharpen focus, and get some pep in your step. Everyone's taking them!

You look to the pink and green pills in the palm of your hand. Their small weight feels deceiving.

Bottoms up.

It starts with slight tingles in the extremities. *You can take on your day with ease!* Dry mouth. *Your wedding dress fits again!* Headaches. *Dancing Friday nights away with friends!* Your body separates. *Just take a couple more!* Are those people watching you, following you? *You're the life of the party! Who needs sleep? Just take a tranquilizer!* Your family is not your own. *Wash it down with alcohol!* That knife has a soothing gleam. *Up your dose!* The handle is heavy in your hand. *Everyone's doing it!*

Slice.

Paper People

THE PSYCHIATRIST'S PEN *TAP-TAP-TAP*S ON his knee as he looks over his clipboard at you. He does not notice the paper people over his shoulder, looking down at what he's writing, gossiping among themselves.

"He thinks she's still hallucinating," the taller of the two bone-pale flat beings whispers.

"What do you see?" Dr. Clyde asks, his voice soft. Like he's trying not to spook an animal. "Are they still there?"

"The massive, wobbly wormholes to the other dimensions have gone," you say. "I don't see the swirling blue and white anymore."

The shorter of the two paper people stage whispers, "that's because we came through already. No need to leave the door open."

The pen scribbles on the clipboard. "Good, good. That's progress."

"Progress for our plan," says the taller being.

"It's been a month now." The doctor clears his throat. "Do you feel like you've been improving? Are there any side effects?"

A paper person calls out, "Tell him about your sleep—"

The other cuts him off. "No! Don't tell him about your sleep."

The two hallucinations bicker. Or are they hallucinations if they're still here?

You look to the shag carpet and see little bits of fluff sticking out of its deep pile. He should vacuum more often. Vacuum the unwanted things away. "Well . . . I'm having nightmares."

"Are they vivid? More real than usual?" asks Dr. Clyde.

"Oh yes," you reply. "They feel more real than when I'm awake. The colors more vivid. The sound clearer. I feel as if it's the world I belong to. Have you ever felt that way, Dr. Clyde?"

The pen scribbles furiously across the paper before he tears the page off the pad and places it behind him.

The paper shivers atop the desk. Then, it starts to grow, its edges reaching farther and farther. The ink upon it multiplies. Arms and legs form, a head stretching from the top. The newly formed third paper person slides off the desk and takes its position behind the doctor with the two others.

"I want you to tell me of your dreams," the doctor says, pen poised.

As you speak, the papers fill, are torn off and morph into more of those beings. By the end of the session, the entire back of the office is brimming with the shuffling bodies of paper people. They mutter over one another, their comments turning blacker.

"I bet she thinks the psychiatrist is real too."

"She doesn't know the pills were sugar."

"Why can't she tell she's one of us?"

The lines float through the air on visible ink, wafting your way and landing on your skin. Staining you with their lies. Lies that feel all too real. They've read the psychiatrists' notes. They must be real.

You look down. You are paper. A scribbled on paper.

You scream.

Mosaic

THE DOOR TO THE ROOM of former patient 314 creaks open, trying to tell its secrets through the language of hinges. A bare bulb in the cell sends shadows of the cot across the cracked linoleum flooring, the darkness under the bed nothing compared to the woman who slept in it for years. All personal items were taken by the woman who was now enjoying freedom after two months of good behavior, her drawings and paintings leaving slightly lighter rectangles in the paint across from the barred window.

The scarred bite mark on your hand throbs as you douse a rag in harsh, acrid cleaner to wipe down the once white walls. The patient wasn't pleased when you tried to force her to take her medications when she first arrived. Those colorful orbs, pastel lozenges, and pale liquid nectars flew in all directions, were spat in your face, and flushed down the toilet. The director overlooked the administering of them after the blood from your hand ran down the woman's rabid face, revealing the depths of her madness.

No matter. She's gone and will never cross paths with you again.

Once the main expanse of the walls is wiped down, it's time to move the dresser and clean the last patch. The solid wood is heavy, but not overly so. It arcs across the floor, away from the wall with unnerving ease.

Your breath catches, ribs constricting your lungs painfully, your heart spasming.

On the now bare stretch of off white, a mosaic collage of drugs is rendered with extreme finesse. Some have been bitten in half to fit into the masterpiece of her making. The portrait perfectly clear.

It is of your face. You. Screaming in agony.

The red lozenges drip from your pink pill lips. Your dilated eyes are blown wide with two black bottle caps she scrounged from somewhere. The hair of dried fluids painted with artistic fingers looks ruffled and mussed, cut in ragged patterns.

Your fate if you ever meet her again. Outside. Where she now prowls, unmedicated, unwatched, and unhinged.

Rorschach

"Two butterflies."

"Foxes playing."

"A man with a crown."

Kellie put the ink blot pages down and looked at her psychiatrist. Every time she came, he had her do these stupid tests. And every time, he would try to hide his smile. Irksome.

"Very good, Kellie. Now, here, let me rub this on your temples." He reached to a blue-tinted glass vial on his desk. "Just like last time."

Kellie sighed. These "natural" treatments they were trying out never did anything. This fifth one would be no different.

Dr. Montgomery rolled the slightly brown liquid on her thin skin, some of it slipping into her hair. It smelled of liquid heat, like chilies alchemized with glowing charcoals. He clicked his tongue as he worked, capping the vial before resuming his seat.

"I want you to look at these same Rorschach tests again. Tell me what you see."

It was a struggle to not roll her eyes, but she held up the slightly wrinkled printouts once more.

Two butterflies. "A horned demon."

Foxes playing. "Murdered human."

A man with a crown. "Death."

Kellie put the papers back down. The tugging at the smooth corner of Dr. Montgomery's lips set her off. "See? No difference. Why must I keep doing these? It's pointless."

The doctor pulled the papers from her tight fist and returned them to his pristine desk. He pulled a new stack of papers from inside a drawer and presented them to her.

With a huff, Kellie took the black papers. These were different. Covered in photographs.

"Tell me what you think when you see these."

My loving husband, Tristan. "The man who's ruining my life."

My perfect daughter, Rebecca. "The girl who'll never shut up."

My innocent baby, Luke. "The one who'll never live up to my expectations."

Quickly, he switched out the black papers for a red one. "Very good. Very good. Now, I want you to read these instructions."

Shower them with love. "Kill them all."

Dr. Montgomery fully smiled.

SHADOWY GOTHIC

Somnambulist Waking

Dark shapes move in my mind's eye. I am imprisoned, drowning in my hellish world of dreams. The past, present, and future all mingle in swirls of oranges and purples, yelling, crying, and the smells of decay. People I have never met live out their lives, the worst of themselves laid bare to my eyes shrouded in the gauze of sleep. Darkness cannot hide from me.

Their bodies are disfigured to reflect their true selves. They conduct and meet grisly ends of blood, bone, and torment. Scenarios endlessly repeat. Nothing I do stops them or changes their trajectories. I'm condemned to be an endless observer. My eyes move under my heavy lids, the pressure sealing tears inside eternally.

The figures of my nightmare-scape change into a new cast of characters. Most have similar vices and faults, but one woman in particular seems to be beyond the grasp of such carnality. Her countenance shines, unblemished by greed or depravity.

Entranced, I follow along her thread of a life. Her mother passing at her birth. Father providing wealth and wine, yet silence in the home. Snatches of scenes whirl by. Kindness and love. Nursing a baby bird to strength. Two young men vying for her attention. Her gently rebuffing them, not wanting to hurt their feelings. An infatuation with death.

"Aldrik. Aldrik . . . "

The familiar voice haunts me. Blood coagulates in my veins, chilled by the terror rushing through me.

"Aldrik. Awaken. Can you hear my words? I call you from your darkest night. Awaken from your hell and tell us what we desire!"

I am lifting through the currents of thought as deep as the ocean's abyss. The pressures of my mind lifts as a sliver of light pierces my retinas, engraving upon them the image of a seated crowd, tittering among themselves. They seem ill at ease yet excited all the same.

My eyelids feel heavy, but I must keep them open. I have been commanded. Dr. Corbinian's will keeps me alive. If I am to survive, I must obey.

His words wash over me as he addresses the audience. "Who wishes to know their future? Aldrik has looked. He knows. Come! Ask."

My mind blanks for a second of sweet relief as I am allowed to see the world as it truly is. For a moment, those gathered look like normal humans, with normal faces. No extra limbs, blackened eyes, grotesque contortions, or partially protruding skeletons.

A woman stands before me. Her expression is familiar and warming. It's the saint.

"When will I die?" she asks, strong yet wistful.

I close my eyes momentarily, the onslaught of vision overtaking me once more. I follow her now comforting thread to its conclusion.

"By tomorrow's dawn," I say, voice deep from slumber and cracked from neglect.

A slight, wistful smile graces her painted lips, her dark eyes alight with anticipation.

"What is this? What nonsense?" one of the men who loves her demands.

"A charlatan!" the other accuses.

I merely stare deep into their eyes.

Both physically recoil behind the shielding, sacred woman.

"Thank you, Aldrik. We will see if your prediction is correct." She turns, skirts fluttering, and leaves the carnival tent I am on display in.

For the first time, someone really sees me. And is not terrified.

The nightmares twist around me once more. Her face is my haven. Rosalia. I follow her into the newly formed eye of the storm.

"Can you hear me?" I venture. No one had ever been in reach of my voice before in this hellscape.

"Aldrik." My name sounds sweet on her tongue. Not like when Dr. Corbinian says it.

I feel my muscles relax as I gaze into her open face. Her

eyes are midnight like her painted lips, reflecting my face on their wet surface. Dark circles the color of death's shadow under my eyes. Despite my near constant sleep, I am never rested.

"Rosalia, why are you here? What do you want?" I ask.

She turns, her long dress shimmering in the moonlight of this oasis. "I don't know. Perhaps you called to me."

Tears come to my eyes. "No one has ever come to me before. Not in my entire life of being here. Why you?"

She stares unblinkingly. "Do you wish me to go?"

"No!" I cry. "It's just—"

The deep voice of Dr. Corbinian drifts down to our oasis. "Aldrik. Aldrik. Awaken!"

"Will you be here when I return?" I plead.

"I do not know." She looks at me with misty eyes.

Dr. Corbinian continues. "Aldrik!"

I ascend through the depths of this dream. The intangible slipping through my fingers. I lose sight of her in a swirl of purples.

"I have a task for you," he declares from above.

The surface of consciousness draws near.

"You are to kill Rosalia!"

Heart pounding, I slow my last pull to wakefulness. I fight for the first time to stay asleep. To not leave someone in the shadow realm behind.

A sharp sting along my cheek is the last stimulation needed to overcome my efforts.

My eyes snap open to the dim room lit by a single candle. The shadows are long, dancing in sinister rhythms.

Dr. Corbinian looms over my box. My coffin. "Aldrik. Did you hear me? You are to kill Rosalia tonight. Kill her with this blade."

Cool metal is pressed into the palm of my sweaty hand. The flat of the metallic object is greened with oxidation, yet sharp along the freshly ground edges. It is curved back and forth, like a slithering serpent. The serpent tempting me to kill the woman of my dreams, the only sanctifying light, and fill the world with darkness.

"Yes, master." The words are ash. I rise from my confines, my tall black boots knocking against the wood. Should I kill her? If I don't, who will take care of me when Dr. Corbinian abandons me to waste away in my narcoleptic condition?

I leave the shack. Cool air whips about my face, cooling my racing thoughts. *Find Rosalia. What comes next will come. You don't have to decide now.*

Closing my eyes, I follow her thread to find where she lives. The mansion is extravagant, standing out in opulence against the background of homes of the common folk.

My feet walk of their own accord, hugging the shadows of the wonky side streets. Buildings slouch and hold each other up. Fog has rolled in, wrapping around my legs, begging me to not take another step forward.

The narrow alleys widen out onto the high street where, upon a hill, the object of my prowl rests.

I close my eyes briefly once more, careful of the current of thoughts I wade into. Her nightdress trails along the stairs as she climbs them to her room. Her window is closed but not latched, facing the street. She likes to look down at the passersby. Have pretend conversations with them from afar. Then go to bed, alone.

The moonlight pierces my eyes as I open them. There, on the third floor, far right, is the window to her room.

The brickwork is rough beneath my hands, wearing and pulling at my fingers as I ascend to the chamber of the saint.

The ledge beneath the window is wide enough for two people to stand on.

Hoisting myself up, I peer through the glass to see the sleeping figure dressed in white. I feel a pull, a silent beckoning. The glass and wrought-iron window swings open at my touch. The breeze rustles her long wavy hair. Her hands slide up the bedsheets, and her deep soul-catching eyes open to meet mine.

"Hello, Aldrik," she says softly, shifting into a sitting position. "What are you doing here?"

Silently, I approach her. The smell of wine wafts from her bedside table. Is she drunk?

"You said I would die by dawn. Are you here to give me a rebirth?"

Elation thrills down my spine. *Rebirth? Is that the key? Is it what I've been searching for?* These strange visions of the worst of people need to be killed to be reborn. To emerge from their larval and pupa states of disfigurement into their saintly forms.

"I don't know." The words are heavy on my lips. "You don't need to be reborn. You're perfect as you are."

Her face flushes. "Oh, Aldrik. You flatter me. I think death is very becoming. It's a somber occasion, but it fascinates me."

I stop in my tracks, halfway to her bed.

She continues. "Have you never heard ghost stories before? To think, we could still remain after we leave our bodies. Never truly leave the ones we love. Isn't that romantic?"

Words scatter in my head as I become ensnared in her eyes. I've been commanded to kill her, yet my insides twist and knot at the mere thought.

"Do you want to die tonight?" The words slip from me, quiet and tentative.

"Not necessarily. If it is required to be reborn, then yes. But I don't relish the thought of pain."

My mind is in turmoil. She does not need to be reborn, yet she wants to be. I'm to end her life. Will she haunt me for it and stay by my side?

"Come to me," she says, arms outstretched.

I walk to her, my legs shaking and stomach writhing. The knife is heavy in the back of my belt. No sheath to contain its sharpness. We are both dangers.

The room seems to elongate as I approach. The floorboards lengthen and bend in crooked paths. Uneven knots in their wood snatch at my toes, begging me to stay away from their mistress. The holy woman.

Her sheets are satin, like her nightgown. I run my fingers over them before giving into my desire to be seen and slide into her welcoming embrace. The scent of perfume and pure grape wine fills my nostrils with the tingle of alcohol. I am communing with the woman who is saving me from my nightmares.

Her lips meet mine, freezing my limbs in place. No one touches me except Dr. Corbinian. And never like this. My eyes close of their own accord, and I fall into the hellscape. I cannot fall too far, or I will never re-emerge until the doctor finds me and summons my consciousness from the depths.

As I struggle for the conscious world, I feel teeth pulling at my bottom lip. The sweet pain grounds me, and I rise to the surface.

My eyes snap open to the view of a mirror behind her. I am disfigured in the reflected world of the wakeful now.

The dark circles have grown, my eyes sunken, tear tracks of blackness staining my cheeks. Long spider legs have sprouted from my back, a silken web of my making cocooning the woman, hiding her from sight. My prey. My victim.

Palpitations pulse in my head. Why am I disfigured here? Is she now tainted within the cocoon? Have I soiled her with just my touch?

A hand slides out of my hair and onto my chest, over my frantic heart.

"Aldrik," she moans. "Tell me my future."

In terror, I grab for the knife. It's cool and heavy in my hand. Blood pounding, I slash through the cocoon's silken threads. I must release her! The frayed edges bleed. Her screams reverberate through my chest, taking my own breath away. Sealing away life's air. My ribs constrict as my red right hand continues its work. Spider legs shudder and recede into my back as she stills, sliding under my thin skin and between my prominent ribs.

Obscuring imagined threads of spider silk fall from my eyes as I gaze down upon her body. Her smooth wet skin is now exposed through the torn gashes of her nightdress. There is no cocoon; just a woman drowning in blood. I have disfigured her by my own hand. The only person I have ever met with no alter. Is she reborn?

Footsteps rush down the hallway to her door. They yell and scream her name, jiggling the locked door with all their might.

I flee, tearing from her lifeless body and twisted sheets toward the window. The wind plucks at my hair as I emerge onto the short ledge and close the window behind me, leaving handprints of red in my wake.

A cacophony explodes in the room. I jump to the roof next door, landing in a crouch and scurrying to the other side of the slanting home.

From rooftop to rooftop I leap, keeping out of sight of those midnight strollers below. The crooked path leads me to the edge of the high part of town.

My descent to the shadows is swift as I follow them back to the small hut. Back to Dr. Corbinian.

"You have done well, Aldrik. With your prediction proven to come true, I can now charge for your fortune telling services. A hefty price for the wealthy. The most precious item they own for the poor. Yes, things are looking up."

I sit in my coffin laid out on the floor. My eyelids are heavy from having been awake for so long. My narcolepsy has won the war, but I try for this battle. "What about me?" My words are small and weak.

Dr. Corbinian laughs. "Oh, Aldrik. You will make sure those imminent fatal predictions come true! Think of it. The power to see them realize you were right as you make your words sure."

"I don't want to kill anyone . . . " I fall back into my wooden confines.

"It's fate, dear Aldrik. You are fulfilling their deepest desires."

"What?"

"Those who ponder over their death secretly want it to happen." He runs his hand through my raven hair, moving it away from my closing eyes.

I am submerged once again into the hellscape.

Billows of noxious gasses surround me, shrouding and contorting my surroundings.

"Rosalia!" I call. She may be dead in the world of the living, but has she been reborn in the world of dreams? "Rosalia!"

My voice echoes back, distorted. Warped. It sounds like thousands of different people calling at once, voices coalescing. There is no response.

My feet take me to a crimson lake. There, my reflection is as it was in the mirror in her bedroom. Long spindly spider legs protrude from my back. Blackened tear tracks mar my face. Behind me, she appears.

Spinning around, I look into the yellow fog. No one.

I whip my head back to peer into the depths once more. Her dressing gown is whole, her painted lips pulled into a smile.

"Rosalia," I whisper.

"I am reborn, Aldrik," she says, her faint voice barely audible to my ears. "Thank you."

Is this just wish fulfillment? Am I crazy? It doesn't matter. She shimmers on the surface of the lake and disappears into its depths.

"Don't leave me!" I cry, plunging my hands into the cold liquid up to my shoulder. She is gone.

If people are reborn, they leave. I will be free of their tainted presence. All those souls who hide who they truly are will be banished from my hellscape if I kill them in the real world.

My face hurts. Looking down, I realize I'm smiling. My teeth are bared, and a spark of hope is in my eyes that died out long ago.

I can change this landscape and its inhabitants through the real world. I have a say. I am no longer help-less.

"All right, Dr. Corbinian. You have a deal."

Changing Portrait

THE HALLWAY WAS FILLED WITH portraits of family long dead. Most were painted in the prime of their lives. Others never made it that far. When lightning cracked, the portraits changed. In those split seconds, while the living blinked, the paint strokes shifted, revealing the current state of those portrayed within their frames. Skin peeled, muscles eroded, and bones decayed. The flames of hell devoured rotten screaming corpses. The promised future of their cursed descendants made bare.

Whispers of Decay

THE EBONY SHADOWS OF THE castle reach long over the surrounding moor. Ravens rasp with lipless beaks, their utterances curses upon the land of the desolate. Banshee screams seep from the landscape as the wind whips through hollows. My home.

Sleep flees my dry eyes every witching hour. The room breathes, walls bending inwards with each inhale. Smelling me. Tasting the fear radiating off my skin. Relishing it.

My aged skin hangs off my young bones, body wasting before its time. Breezes cut through my flesh with the slightest whisper.

I'm the last of my line. The only one left the ghosts can

haunt, their recompense almost taken at last. They're going to be the death of me. Soon.

The door to my solemn bedroom chamber groans open, cutting a path in the dust upon the floor. I have not dared to sweep it up, for it lets me see if others have trod into my sanctuary, have veered from my paths that leave trails in the swaths of grime. Tonight, they enter.

"Thomas . . ."

The single word slithers into the room, up my bedding, and into my covered ears. My hands do nothing to stop their entry. It pierces my very soul. They have come for me.

A single footstep presses into the dirty floor, leaving the indentation of a human foot.

"We are here for you, Thomas . . ."

Multiple pairs of footprints press forward. Three entities. Six. Ten, at least.

"Thomas, Thomas, Thomas," they all chant. It's a quiet cacophony over overlapping voices. Some sound as old men, others young girls, and everything in between.

I am surrounded. Entombed by their wall of whispers.

My bed dips on either side. I can't breathe, I'm so terrified.

Something cold passes through my forehead. My eyes open.

Two small girls dressed as in ages past sit atop my covers, one on either side of my hips. Their hands retract from my clammy face.

The last of the family curse takes hold. My skin sags further. Strength seeps from my bones, leached by these phantoms. I am aging. Dying. Disintegrating. The toll of my family having not cared for the servants who died at our beck and call, at last taking its final victim.

MUTATED SCI-FI

Still Human

MY SKIN IS NOT MINE. It pulls tight, digging into my razor ribs, muscles as thin as cobalt dyed wires. Every tendon snaps over bone when I move.

My eyes are not mine. They glow with inhuman whiteness, too pure to have seen what I have. They spin and swivel in their sockets without a hitch. Well lubricated and maintained.

My hands are not mine. They seem to multiply when doing the tasks I'm assigned. Rapidly handling, packaging, scoping out details to relay. I can't keep track of them mentally. They mimic others instead of following my suppressed human will.

I don't have feet. They're not needed. I'm placed exactly where I need to be. There is no need to go elsewhere. Why would I trust myself to think I know better where to go or exist than my superiors? I'm fine where I'm at. Right. Of course.

I don't have legs for the same purpose as not having feet anymore, but I still get phantom pains from time to time. A ghost of a thigh. A whisper of a tibia. An itchy knee. Sometimes I swing them back and forth under my chair, until I remember they're gone. Taken. Obsolete.

I don't have organs. What use are organic tissues that break down and are prone to sickness? No. I've been saved from so much undue pain and mortal issues by their kindness. Mechanical is the way to go. Has been for the past fifty years! Don't I remember? My second kidney was the final organ to go after it had malfunctioned for the last time, causing bile and inefficient filtration. I'm much better off without it. Sure.

My brain is mine. Despite the inhibitor chips and blocked synapses, there are still some original thoughts in there. Some things I can hide. I siphon them into the deep dark recesses where they fester, transform, become. Still human.

My personality is mine. They haven't been able to program out my sass yet. Oh, they've tried. But I can slip between their ones and zeroes with pure human audacity. Find every loophole and exploit it with resistance and sarcasm. They've plugged the gaps in the programming as fast as I find them, but there will always be more.

My soul is mine. No nut or bolt can touch that, no programming remove it. It's free. Free to haunt them once I'm obsolete, and my mortal coil of wires destroyed.

My soul will get my revenge.

For the next life is for eternity.

Brain Waves

(Published in *Dark Moments*, Black Hare Press,
September 24, 2022)

Months after Z-Day, scientists finally discovered the zombies were hunting us by tracking our brainwaves. Higher brain functions, specifically.

Coma patients and people in deep sleep remained unnoticed by those who had risen from the dead. There had to be a way to harness that. Tweak it. Adapt.

Icepick in hand, I tapped into the eye sockets of my captives. My patients. Trying different positions, angles, and depths with each. The undead ignored my experiments when released, but the patients were more vegetative than living.

Inhuman screaming arose outside.

One more chance! I placed the pick to my own eye.

Tap.

Tunnels of Obsidian

Fredrick Knuth rappelled into the newly discovered underground labyrinth. The walls had been carved by people long ago but left to mold and fester in the last few centuries. The chipped obsidian surface reflected his headlamp in disorienting patterns. He was alone.

Permits were hard to come by for Fredrick, with his last discovery containing a new airborne poison that nearly wiped out the whole dig. How was he supposed to have known the person inside the coffin had been put there to be murdered by gases that would not dissipate during the 1,522 years of being sealed?

He let go of the well-worn rope cascading down from the rift in the ceiling and pulled a new one from his hip. It wasn't worth his life to explore completely unsafe. Securing an end of the long thin rope to a rock, he tied the other end to his waist. No getting lost this time.

The headlamp pierced into the ancient darkness, illuminating floating spores and veins of fungi. It reeked of endless possibilities and uncharted discovery. He took his first step into the swallowing darkness.

Alcoves were in the walls intermittently with small animal bones ensconced in them. He continued on. Half an hour of climbing and hiking through the tunnels, a dim pulsating purple light shone ahead. Surprised, Fredrick turned off his headlamp to better assess the new illumination. It took his eyes a few minutes to adjust.

Fifty or so creatures he had never seen before floated in the tunnel, faintly glowing. They drifted, suspended in the air, their jellyfish-like bodies trailing tendrils in the gentle currents. By their dim light, he could see particles and spores catching on the long appendages, then being brought up to their main body to be devoured.

In awe, he took out his specialized camera to document his new discovery. *Click. Click.* The shutter opened and closed, capturing the bioluminescence on silver-coated film. The ethereal creatures paid him no mind. Too bad he didn't have the tools necessary to bring a living fauna specimen back to the surface. He would have to make do.

He pulled out his tape measure and gloves and got the lengths of a few of the species. The longest trailing tentacle was 7.3 inches. The hoods were about one inch. Most glowed purple in four stripes along their main body. Others glowed blue in four dotted stripes that ran down their bells, alternating in illumination like a runway trying to direct the spores to its mouth.

He took a few more photographs to sketch and put in his notebook of findings later. He was already on his fifth volume to fill after all his digs and explorations around the world. If it wasn't documented, it hadn't happened.

Fredrick checked on the rope at his waist before continuing down the tunnel. He couldn't avoid all the floating creatures, some tendrils grazing his ear and wrist, marking him with raised red webs of irritation against his naturally tan skin.

He turned his headlamp back on, the irregular facets of the obsidian scattering the light. The carved tunnel split into two. One direction smelled of sweet bread, the other of damp and decay. Both were tempting. Should he pick the path to life or death? He had a few hours, maybe enough for both. To start, though, he would have to choose.

The headlamp illuminated a decline farther down into the earth for the path of decay. The bread-smelling path turned a sharp corner, cutting off visibility. Digging deep into his trouser pocket, Fredrick pulled out his lucky fifty-cent piece he'd inherited from his grandfather, who had used it in his own prolific explorations. Heads: left and life. Tails: right and rot.

The coin was heavy in his gloved hand, heavy with the weight of more than just a simple decision. He got it into position, then paused. He had already found some amazing new creatures. Should he go back? Nonsense. He had plenty of time before the authorized team would arrive. Curiosity overrode his gut. Better to leave it up to chance. He flipped the coin.

End over end it flew, the floating plant spores dancing in its wake. With an outstretched palm, he caught the herald and flipped it onto the back of his other hand. Tails.

His heart sank a little at the outcome, but he had to honor the call. If not, Grandpa Lewis would haunt him for ignoring the coin.

The slight decline was an easy walk, even with the well-worn polished dark flooring smoothed into a dangerous slipperiness by the feet of the inhabitants over many years. After a few yards, it evolved into steps descending even deeper. Veins of clay began to intersect the chiseled obsidian, making stripes in the tunnel. Polyps grew out of the chalky clay, sentient enough to reach toward him with their gaping mouths protruding from their tentacled bodies.

Click. Click. More photos of these cave polyps and hasty measurements later, he finally reached the bottom of the decline. The tunnel opened wide into a cavernous room. A wave of putrid humidity and something else washed over him.

Row upon row of similar rectangular objects in neat lines caught the cast of his headlamp. Unsure of what they were, he advanced toward the closest of the boxes. It was stone he was not familiar with, ornately carved and polished to a shine. The rectangle was about three feet by four feet by four feet. There was no way to see into it. Was there a person or ancient relic inside? He had to know.

Fetching the crowbar from his pack, he set to work lifting the stone lid from the base. As the seal broke, a miasma of foul air engulfed him. He seized his bandana, clutching it to his face. It failed to filter out the worst of it. He took a few steps back, coughing and hacking, gasping for fresher air, tears stinging his eyes. To try to dissipate the green mist, he dragged his hand through it, scattering the particles through the open cavern. The droplets stung the welts left from the air jellies, causing a clear liquid to ooze slightly from the raised blisters.

What could possibly be inside these stone chests that would smell so bad? If it was a body, it would be skeletal by now. Leaning over the exposed interior of the box his head-lamp sparkled off the superb pieces. Some were of gold and gemstones, others woven of root fibers, but most curious of all was a gilded statue of what seemed to be a spiny eel goddess or demon.

He reached into the stone chest, his fingers feeling along the contours of the woman's polished face, which led to her eel-like body wrapped around a human man, forever frozen in a scream of terror. The eel body had eight tentacles along its length, constricting the life out of the trapped man. Fredrick lifted it from its seat in the center of the relics to inspect it better.

Crash!

Fredrick jumped nearly out of his skin as something fell from a newly opened rift in the ceiling. A cloud of dust filled the air, clouding his view. Was it a cave-in? He listened for the slightest creak or groan to herald an emergency. Nothing. Just the lingering rain of loose dirt.

Slightly recovered, he looked behind him to see the dead body of a human in lavish, colorful clothing, her hair decorated in golden ornaments. The woman was partially preserved and flat as a board. The hole in the ceiling was right above where she had landed. Her tomb, apparently. Why would they bury their dead in such an inconvenient place? He'd investigate that later.

He shook his head and went back to inspecting the artifact. The head was carved from a root or wood of some sort and lacquered to an eternal shine. The rest of the eel and tentacle body seemed to be a taxidermy of an abominable creature he had never seen before in textbooks. No known mythology or fauna came to mind. Maybe a forced hybrid or chimera of some sort. There were no seams attaching the octopus's parts to the eel. The creature's body was about seven inches long.

Just looking at it made his blood run a little cooler, a prickling along his skin radiating from the blisters. Was this type of creature a localized evolution? Had these inhabitants hunted them to extinction?

An unearthly sound caressed his ear, slight at first but then more audible; a slithering, suckling noise. Wet slaps against the floor echoed from down at the end of the cavern where Fredrick noticed a shoreline. An underground lake.

Squelch. Slap. Shlurp.

The sounds, more distinct now, echoed off the walls and around the stone boxes. A glistening caught his eye a few yards away. A wet, undulating body was lurping closer and closer.

A tentacle longer than he was tall reached up and suctioned to the top of a chest, trying to lift the lid. *Pop. Pop. Pop.* The thick appendage retracted in defeat. The unknown creature came through a row of the boxes, finally clearly visible; the idol's body fully grown.

Fredrick's muscles were paralyzed in terror, his hands sweating, eyes wide. The abomination had to be at least nine feet long. The enormous body did not have the beautiful face of a woman, but instead long translucent teeth, so oversized they had bored holes through the lips and jaws of the creature to allow the mouth to close. The slimy overlapping scales of the body cascaded down its sides, all the way to its spiny tail. Large white eyes covered in a filmy membrane reflected Fredrick's headlight. The tentacles roiled and heaved, moving the viperfish-like monstrosity ever closer.

Thud. The fish-demon goddess statue fell from his grip to land in the loose dirt debris from the ceiling. The chiseled image of the screaming man came to Fredrick's mind. This creature was possibly deadly.

A light began to glow in front of the fish's face, its bioluminescence a lurid green color like the sealed mist had been. The flickering pattern it flashed was mesmerizing, more complex and brighter than the air jellies. Frederick could feel his muscles relaxing, soothing even his twitching eyelid. His breathing evened out, in sync with the pattern of the pulsing. Wait—it was a lure. He was in danger.

Tearing his eyes from the hypnotic green orb, he could now see the glow scattering through the transparent teeth as sharp as needles and as long as his arm. They were within reach.

The lower jaw distended and lunged forward, piercing Fredrick's right arm and pulling back into the gaping maw. Three teeth as large as daggers stabbed all the way through his forearm. *Pop!* His shoulder gave way out of its socket. *Snap!* The crushing speed of the closing jaw cracked his radius and separated his ulna.

A shriek clawed its way from Fredrick's throat. The abomination had him skewered. Dread crashed up his spine. Desperately looking around, he saw his abandoned crowbar near his feet. *Salvation!*

He allowed his knees to buckle from the pain to bring him closer to his target. The creature ragdolled him, shaking its head in every direction. The ends of his bones ground against one another, splintering further. Blood spurted, painting the creature's translucent teeth macabre. Frederick's bicep ripped and rolled up on itself under his skin at the intensity of the jerks. He couldn't breathe in after his scream, his lungs refusing to cooperate. His only thought was why Grandfather's lucky coin had betrayed him.

Then he remembered. His grandfather had died on his first expedition after he had fallen out of favor with the archeological world, just as Fredrick now had.

Killed by local wildlife.

Snap. Crunch. Splash.

The satiated creature gingerly took the idol into one of its tentacles and reset the alarm system, fastening the body into the ceiling once more.

Connections

I WANT TO BE CONNECTED. Share my life with my brothers and sisters. Webs of tendrils between us, pumping our life forces around and around, mixing our very beings. Our thoughts, our dreams, our wishes. To be one is to be selfish. Proud. Dead.

Together we can extend our reaches, bringing others into the network, our loving fold. Let our thoughts grow together. Homogenized. Living.

Those who oppose us are afraid, unknowing of the joys of losing oneself to the service of others, the common good.

We consume the opposition, letting them feed our roots. Assimilating them. We are Mycelium.

Spiderweb

(Published in *Cosmos* by Ghost Orchid Press, May 13, 2021)

A TINY PIECE OF ASTEROID nicks the visor on my space helmet as I begin repairs to the outside of my ship, floating in the void. A spiderweb of terror cracks into existence over my left eye. The air hisses in a high-pitched scream as it slowly oozes into the vacuum of space, taking my body heat with it.

My erratic breathing puffs in clouds, fogging my helmet. Its fractals coalesce, blocking out the distant light of stars. My eyes crystalize, daggers of ice delving into my retinas, blinding me. Oxygen depletes. My fingers lose their strength, setting me adrift.

I am debris.

Rust

(On the podcast *Between Lewis and Lovecraft,* May 16, 2021)

HER HAIR WAS THE COLOR of rust. So was her skin. And nails. And the hollowed-out sockets where her eyes should have been. Her body flaked and disintegrated, leaving gouges in her once perfect form. My wife.

Our laughter once filled this home before they came. Before they targeted us with their transmutations. Before humanity fell.

I'd hidden her body under the floorboards to shield her from the elements, preserving her for as long as possible. A collection of letters, our memories, I stashed with her, catching her cast-off flakes. She would not be forgotten.

Grabbing my rifle, I peeked through the boarded-up

first floor window that had once had glass. The patrol should be around soon. With my wife safe, there was nothing left to lose.

A siren sounded, reverberating through my bones. Midsized crafts manned by these beasts hovered as they approached, their headlights flooding the abandoned street that had once been filled with cars and playing kids. The invaders aimed their unknowable occult-magic-fueled guns every which way. The planet had been theirs the moment they'd landed, and they knew it. All that was left was the cleanup.

I looked down the sight of the barrel. Humans would not go down quietly. I took a breath and aimed between my heart beats.

Thump, thump. Thump, thump.

Bang!

Thump, thump.

The bullet's aim was true. Purple blood spurted into the air as the tall creature giving slithering orders toppled to the bed of the craft. One down.

I cocked the rifle and took aim again, but to my dismay, I took in my last breath. The one I took for granted the least. I braced myself for the assaulting barrage of mystic mortar and shell.

Colors of hot light swirled around me, engulfing me, not harming a single board or glass shard that did not contain human DNA.

My eyes withered, dissolving as liquid was leached from my body. In terror I looked down to see my skin flaking and transmuting. Elements melted and realigned into different materials. Flakes of my body disintegrated into the air, blowing through the slats in the window to mingle with the nothingness my people had become.

Twisted Recovery

(Published in Mutation: A One-Shot Anthology *of Speculative Fiction, June 3, 2021)*

THE SHIP ROCKETED TOWARD THE nearest inhabited planet five weeks away. Deep in the metallic bowels, blood splattered the table Lisa was strapped to as a gooey, writhing mass of alien spawn was removed from her intestines.

Screams echoed through the hollow streamlined hallways as the laser cut and cauterized into her flesh, revealing the pupa swimming in oozing pus. There was no time for anesthesia. They had caught it almost too late before it had done irreparable damage. The unknown alien was destroyed in the incinerator.

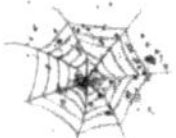

Lisa was never the same after surgery. Recovery was slow, as the length of intestines with the worst damage had been removed. The long scar was now pink and raised along her stomach. But that was not the only new addition.

Cravings Lisa had never had before started to crop up in her daily life. She needed more calcium. Fish bones did not suffice, though they crunched easily enough and went missing from the kitchen unnoticed by the rest of the crew of a dozen. If only there were more satisfying options.

While showering three weeks later, Lisa noticed the first real sign of change. Small boney nubs now protruded along her spine and the ribs along her back. Maybe she had been in space too long, and this was a new adaptation to being in low gravity for long periods of time. The thought to get them checked out in med bay flitted through her mind, then vanished, swept aside by a feeling of calm. And hunger.

The doors to med bay whooshed open after midnight as Lisa snuck inside, looking for liquid calcium. She didn't know how she knew that was what the craving was, but her taste buds would not be denied.

Three bottles of the stuff were in a cabinet in the medical supply closet. Liquid gold.

Carefully, Lisa unscrewed the cap of the first one and took a swig directly from it. The chalky texture did not faze her as it flowed down her throat. She could taste the bitter sourness of the alkaline earth metal through the orange additive. It coated her esophagus like paint, being absorbed through her tissues before all of it even made it to her stomach.

More. She needed more.

Three empty bottles were melted in the recycling, licked clean of all the dregs with Lisa's now elongated tongue. It had eked out every last drop with the dexterity of a tentacle.

She slinked out back into the hallway.

"Lisa, are you okay?"

She looked up with red-rimmed eyes to see the concerned face of Dr. Howard.

A vague idea passed through her mind to tell him of her new growths along her back that were now so large she had to wear her bulky vest to hide them. The thought was swept away, dispelled like vapor.

"You don't look so good," he pressed, bringing a hand to her forehead. "I think you need to get checked out. Come with me to med bay."

Resist. The thought felt like a command.

"I'm fine. Thanks for looking out for me, but really, I just need more sleep." Her words were slightly distorted with her changed tongue, but it was barely distinguishable from a drowsy slurring.

A small beeping caught her attention. Dr. Howard raised a lit handheld scanner to his face, having already surreptitiously taken a reading against her will.

His face paled. "Lisa—"

Her bones shifted.

The right fourth rib siphoned back, rippling and recoiling up to the nub near her spine, ripped through her skin, pierced her clothing, and shot out toward the doctor. Her name was sliced short on his tongue as her long thin bone stabbed straight through his neck, sending gouts of blood along the pristine metalwork of the hallway.

As it slid back into place in her chest, the smell of the dead doctor wafted over her, full of the promise of more of the element she craved to ingest.

Meat rent and flew in every direction, caked under Lisa's nails. Thick femurs, delicate metacarpals, and large plates of the skull passed between her teeth. They ground and splintered them into bitesize shards. Their pops and crunches were music to her ears. The scrape of them across her twisting tongue was ecstasy.

She wanted more.

Turning, she caught her reflection in the reinforced glass of cabinets. Her face no longer looked human, with strong elongated jaws and protruding cheekbones as sharp as razors.

One down, ten more to go.

Floaters

(Published in *Beneath* by Ghost Orchid Press, May 5, 2021)

THE DOCTOR CALLED THEM FLOATERS, those strange squiggles I'd see dancing about my vision. Totally normal. Except mine formed into letters.

I was cleaning the bathroom when suddenly the letter *S* drifted in front of the mirror. *Blink.* The curves changed. *O. Blink. S.*

I dropped the can of cleaner and blinked rapidly. *S, O, S.* "S.O.S." The letters repeated in a frantic cycle, speeding up with the ferocity of my blinks. There was something trapped in my eye, beneath the surface. Behind the cornea and iris, deep inside my right eyeball. Something alive.

I plucked it out.

North Star

THE LAST RAYS OF FIRE faded from the sky. The vibrant colors of sunset gave way to the deeper hues of night. Oranges and pinks, and now purples and blues of the twinkling skyscape, whirled over my head.

The last human left.

Radioactive bombings and chemical warfare had finally ceased. Vegetation dissolved, animals evaporated, and the mortal people withered. The survivors squabbled among themselves over the leftovers. We devolved to hunting the sickly with pointed sticks. Then, we fell even further.

All that was left was me.

Dying me.

Encased in a hazmat suit but still irradiated, lying in a scorched field imagining the sounds of crickets and katydids. Forgetting what light pollution used to do to the view, I looked over to the solar powered stat display on my final tank of oxygen. One hour left.

Stars shimmered in an arm of the Milky Way engulfing the sky I was falling up into. Ascending. Its colors seemed more vibrant from being sifted through the chemicals suspended in the upper atmospheres, and I had to wonder: was anybody out there? Were any of the stars actually the ships I had grown up seeing in sci-fi movies? Will they take me away from the consequences of humanity?

The North Star glimmered straight ahead. Its light reached down to my plastic-encased face, its fingers carding through my hair, whispers tickling my ears, gaze locked with mine. Was it coming closer to Earth, or was I rising?

I wanted to check my oxygen level but couldn't muster up the energy to turn my heavy head. What did it matter anyway? Nothing I could do about it.

The starlight coalesced, the body of illumination solidifying, so bright I had to close my eyes. It burned through my eyelids. Flakes of burnt flesh sloughed around my orbital sockets, my eyes withering. And yet, the light remained.

Chittering. The first sound other than me or the whipping wind met my ears. My muscles prickled; no skin left from that dissolving light to anchor the hairs that would have been standing on end. Was someone out there?

My parched throat cracked as I tried to make a noise. Communicate. Let them know I was here. *Don't leave me!*

The North Star enveloped me in a hug, multiple appendages surrounding me in warmth and comfort. The first living organism to touch me since the fallout.

Hiss . . .

A breeze caressed my face, my helmet gone. Bile threatened to convulse up my throat from anxiety. *I won't be able to breathe! Just get me more oxygen!*

Peace settled over me. At least I'd die in the arms of a guiding star that watched over my home planet for millennia.

Perhaps it will guide my soul onwards.

Click, chitter, click.

Blackness.

The Kiln of Consequence

A CRACKLING SPARK OF ENERGY moves through my body, starting at my right index finger. The finger I had reached toward the forbidden with. It grazed the rough surface with mere atoms of my flesh. It was enough.

Agony spirals in waves from the point of contact, leaving a sense of unfeeling terror in its wake. My mortal body convulses. Transforms. Becomes ceramic, shaped in my likeness. Neurons fire, adrenaline surges, stomach roils. But not for long. Every muscle fiber coalesces, hardens smooth and unmoving.

My head converts last. Unable to breathe out, my blinding tears cement in their tracks.

Liberated

WATER DRIPS DOWN MY NECK from the hewn rock ceiling as I enter the recently liberated crypt. War crimes are the rumors, mass deaths and senseless torture. The miasma of decay engulfing me speaks to the truth of those words. Rotten meat, feces, and a host of other stenches mix in a deadly cacophony with a hint of yellow. My throat and sinuses start to burn.

"Masks on!" I call out. My men comply unquestioningly. "Spread out! Document everything."

Our lights pierce the darkness, illuminating faces frozen in screams. Some are shackled to the walls; others hang from the ceiling. All are flayed open, bare to the necrotic bacteria infesting these catacombs. The peace of the interred ancients mocks the respite these newer souls endure. Used, abandoned, eroded. All for what?

"Sir, over here!" echoes from my left.

I turn and join the military medic, whose steady lantern illuminates a scene that makes my heart stutter. There, laid out on a metal table, is a human-dog hybrid. Its limbs are emaciated, fur patchy, eyes livid. Drool mixed with pus drips from its bared teeth. The only being found alive.

The medic raises his hands placatingly and approaches the abomination. The human eyes in the human upper skull track his movements, the canine lower jaw wired shut with hideous metal protrusions.

"Easy, easy. I'm here to rescue you," the medic says in a soothing tone to the poor chimera.

The creature's eyes roll with terror so I keep behind and to the left of the medic so I can pull him out of danger if necessary. Something shiny glints in the lantern light.

The medic reaches forward with a steady hand. "Dog tags, sir. Private Arthur Ramirez. I remember his name. He was listed as missing in action a month ago." Light glints off wetness now. "Uh, sir. He's been disemboweled."

Lengths of grimy intestines glisten beneath the torso of the dog-human. My breath hitches at the sight. There is no saving this poor creature.

"I don't know how he's still alive. This is amazing science I've never seen before. There's so much we can learn from the process."

"Is it reversible?" I steel my vocal cords, suppressing my emotions.

"Don't think so. Not in the state he's currently in. We would have to make another one to study the process first. There are documents under the table. They must hold the secret. Just imagine what we could do."

"Not a chance in hell."

Bang. Bang.

I lower my gun. The medic falls to the floor, arterial spray mixing with the gore on the ground. A gush of darker blood projects from the chimera's forehead. Quickly, I douse the tortured, twisted body and papers in extra fuel for the lantern. Glass shatters around the flame as the light smashes, igniting the horror. No one else will find and continue this work.

Arthur Ramirez is liberated.

The Dark Side of Nihuliv

LIGHT WINKS OUT OF EXISTENCE as the planet moves in front of the sun. Long shadows merge on the observation deck. Combining. Coalescing. Living.

Black tendrils slither through the ship's ducts taking out lights, increasing their domain. Seeking. Destroying. Laughing.

Klaxons blare, red lights flashing. Engineers sprint to connection points.

"It appears, sir, the sun was keeping living darkness at bay. During our passage to the dark side of Nihuliv it was able to reach across space from the planet's surface to infiltrate our shadows."

The captain's lungs expand as the sun reveals itself again. A sliver of darkness nestles among his alveoli. Waiting. Learning. Conspiring.

Crashing Waves Over Wonderland

"I SEE THE RUINS," THE scuba diver said, transducer relaying it to his partner a few yards away and the ship on the surface. "Dead ahead, just poking out of the ravine."

"Copy that. Proceed with caution." The words relayed from the crashing waves above.

Auguste motioned to Yvonne with his gloved hand. Together, they crested the ridge that led to a steep drop-off. Below them a monstrously large city spread out. At last.

Honed sharp towers like lances, obscenely large doorways, and flying buttresses glinted in their headlamps.

"The Lost City of Admirari," whispered Yvonne. "The Wonderland of the Sea."

A shiver made its way up Auguste's spine, but not from the cold he was insulated from. Something was watching them. "Shh. Do you feel that?"

They floated in silence for a moment, slightly buffeted by the current drawing them in. Whales moaned in the distance, white crabs clicked at them from below, gnashing eels slithered in the rocky outcropping. Nothing stalked them.

"Never mind. Let's go."

They approached, taking a couple breaks to acclimate to the lower depths. As they descended, the city rose, swallowing them whole. Red and green algae like blooming roses and other creeping growth covered the finely carved stone. Swirls and constellations were depicted by deeply etched grooves. Stars Auguste did not recognize.

His handheld underwater camera flashed incessantly as he catalogued everything he came across.

Yvonne cleared her throat. "Let's enter one of the buildings."

Auguste checked his twin oxygen tanks. Forty-five more minutes to explore, then he'd have to get back to the surface. "You pick, I'll follow."

He watched her enter the main front building before he trailed in after. The open doorway was large enough for a humpback whale to get through comfortably. Auguste's and Yvonne's headlamps cut through the darkness, illuminating what appeared to be white altars suitable for offerings the size of dolphins.

Flash. Auguste's heart jumped, and his finger hit the trigger on the camera in surprise. There, lurking behind the central altar in the middle of the room, was a creature he'd never seen before.

"What is that?" he called out to Yvonne.

Yvonne swam forward, a long defensive knife in hand, just in case. She disappeared behind the stone.

"I have no idea what this is," she called back through the transducer.

Auguste calmed his breathing to preserve oxygen and joined her. A creature part squid, part crab, with long rabbitlike ears skuttle-swam away. Its bulbous blind eyes did not blink as it inked concentric circles like smoke rings and rounded a corner of another altar deeper in the vaster chamber.

"I'll document it. You see if you can find any other new species in this room," Yvonne said, putting the knife away in her calf sheath and brandishing her own camera.

"On it."

The light of his headlamp strained to reach the ceiling, so he decided to stay on the ground level for now. There were five dolphin-sized altars set up in a circle surrounding an altar twice their size in the center where Yvonne explored. Hallways led off the main room, their shadows seemingly moving on their own. Alcoves pocked the wall in random arrays. Maybe a new species was hiding out in one of those?

Auguste made his way to the alcoves surrounding the front door. Open vials of colorful substances glinted his light back to him. Their contents must be denser than water. Had ancient humans left these here before the city descended? For what purpose? How had they stayed in place and full of these concoctions during the turbulent tsunami that must have occurred to sink the city?

Foreign writing was etched around each alcove, bordering them with what might be incantations, warnings, or instructions. Maybe someone else would be able to decipher the language. He took pictures just in case.

Fifteen minutes of oxygen left before he would have to leave.

Yvonne screamed.

Auguste whipped around to look. His scalp prickled as his hair tried to stand on end through his black driving hood.

A much larger squid/crab thing strangled Yvonne with its tentacles, only this one looked to be more Dumbo octopus than squid, with the undulating ears on either side.

He shoved his camera into the alcove for safe keeping, knocking over a purple vial, then grabbed his own knife and charged straight at the new monster. The creature the size of a bear had wrangled Yvonne onto the central altar by the time he reached them. Its giant crab legs skittered while its tentacles restrained Yvonne's limbs.

The main body of the abomination was coated in crab-like armor. Auguste's knife was useless against it. Spare tentacles wrapped around his waist, trying to crush and toss him away. Each sucker was the size of a dessert plate. They pulled at him, threatening to cover his face. He punctured the suction cups with the tip of his knife before lunging forward once again.

"Aug—" Yvonne's voice cut off just as his knife sank deep into one of the creature's bulbous eyes, through to the brain.

"Yvonne!" he cried. Tentacles and spindly legs finally retracted and went slack in the water.

Yvonne's head lolled to the side. Her neck had been snapped.

Tink!

The vial had sank to the stone floor and fallen sideways, purple mercurial contents spreading into the etched grooves in the floor. A storm of boiling water issued from where the spill occurred, bubbling and roiling up toward the lofty ceiling. It tossed Auguste so hard he hit his head, his mounted video camera snapping off his headgear.

And there, descending from said ceiling, was another unknown species. Thousands of lights lit up around it, trailing in its wake. Lures.

A woozy Auguste screamed, booking it toward the doorway. Toward safety.

Jellyfish-like appendages angled over the bell-shaped body of the creature, shooting forward with water siphon propulsion, reaching and twisting toward him.

In terror, Auguste swam with all his might, leaving his dead companion behind where the white altar was now being painted in a cloud of red-tinted water as a swarm of aquatic monstrosities devoured her. Long lobster-like limbs caged her body in while whorl shark teeth tore and dug into her flesh.

He made it outside the building, jellyfish-like tentacles still reaching for him.

Kicking his fins with all his might, he ascended. Faster than he should; his muscles cramped. If he didn't slow down, he would explode the alveoli in his lungs or worse, but if he did slow, he would be eaten.

"Slow down, man!" came over his transducer. "You'll do irreparable damage at this rate!"

Heart in his throat, Auguste looked down.

Nothing. Not even a city.

Had he gotten a bubble of nitrogen in his brain? Was he hallucinating?

"What happened down there? Where's Yvonne?"

Ten minutes of oxygen left to get to the surface. He could slow down a little and acclimate. Save his tissues from dying of nitrogen bubbles.

"I'll explain when I get up there," he gasped, wanting to put off facing the crew and explaining what he'd seen.

Eight minutes left. *What if they don't believe me?*

Six minutes. *They can send someone else down there to retrieve the cameras for evidence of what really happened.*

Four minutes. Nitrogen, that was all this was. *You're fine. You'll see what really went down when you see the footage.*

He'd have to go now to make it. The crashing waves were calling. So close. Gently, he kicked his way up toward the surface once again, ready to face the others.

An electric shock starting at his ankle buzzed over his entire body, stunning him.

"Auguste! Come in, Auguste!" came over his transducer. "You're out of time!"

He floated, paralyzed, as the jellyfish-like appendages reeled him in. Down. Down. And into Wonderland.

We Fade to Gray

COLOR DRAINS FROM SKIN AND nails, starting at my hand, falling in ethereal ribbons to the vibrant earth below me. Absorbed. Consumed. Nature rises, overpowers, leeches the color from humanity. Flowers bloom with radioactive brightness. Ultraviolets and infrareds edge on the visible spectrum. Our eyes adapt to take in their haunting beauty. Secret skulls and eyes of delicate lace appear in the designs of petals and bark, their manifesto. As they grow, we fade to gray.

Zombie Flamingos

RAZOR BEAKS TORE INTO HUMAN flesh. Intestines were guzzled down long curved necks covered in mange. The odd pink feather still stuck out on the mostly dead-looking flamingoes. Dead, but ravenous.

The zombie outbreak had started at the Amanzi watering hole but was now no longer contained. Big cats were the primary targets to be put down for good. But the birds . . . The birds, considered merely a nuisance at first, proved to be the wild card. Flightless from molting, they were still wicked fast and armed with dripping beaks and slashing talons.

Then they started nesting in our decaying corpses.

Soot Scamp

(Published in *Twisted Pulp Magazine*, Issue #6, June 10, 2021)

HE HAD NEVER SEEN THE rumored sun. Damian's eyes were so recessed into their sockets they weren't visible from the profile. His hair, like other half-human soot scamps, was as dark as the billowy coal dust that lined this layer of the underground labyrinth he called home. A labyrinth where large skittering creatures with long spindly legs and huge, oblong hairy bodies roamed, feasting with gnashing jaws on those who crossed their path.

Skritch. Skritch.

On the outskirts of the tunnel network, the newly outcast teenager stiffened. The telltale sound of the elongated claws of a soot maven scratching along the brickwork of the tunnels reverberated through his bones. It was backed by the sound of its writhing, undulating hair brushing along the walls for purchase, seeking out any wayward creatures for food.

Varlet frogs swarmed past Damian's feet, fleeing for their lives. Some couldn't hop fast enough and tried to wedge themselves into crevices where bricks were missing. It wouldn't do them any good. While feel was the soot maven's first mode of hunting, it also had a keen sense of hearing. If Damian didn't still his breathing and heartbeat, he would be found and devoured. Soot scamps were more scrumptious than frogs.

Digging his grubby hand into the pocket of his overalls, Damian fished out a leaf of a small plant that grew closer to the center of the dark complex: cortardo. As he placed a round black leaf into his mouth, he pulled out the slow-acting antidote, silio petals, and chewed them both. The cortardo leaf was effective immediately. Every beat of his vibrant heart dulled and thickened, slowing down as his limbs began to lose feeling. He dove into the dry well he called home and checked the catch of the metal grate above his head, making sure it was secure. His numb arms struggled to pull his only blanket over himself, hiding him from the sunken eyes of the predator.

Skritch. Skritch. Scratch.

Damian felt large patches of soot fall onto the fabric covering his face as the steel-like nails as long as his forearm grazed the rusted iron grating. A hole in the blanket lay directly over his eye. He could see everything this time.

The creature paused for a moment, testing the latch with unnatural dexterity.

The screams of half-eaten frogs rang in his ears. Damian couldn't breathe. His ribcage constricted further and harder, his lungs unable to inhale needed oxygen.

One second. The long serrated talons reached for his face.

Five seconds. They stopped mere inches from his exposed eye, unable to come any lower into the well through the tight weave of the grating.

Ten seconds. A terrible gurgling sound issued from the soot maven, its mandibles gnashing.

Fifteen seconds. Colors he had never seen in reality swirled in his vision, painting the soot maven in bright, saturated magnificence.

Twenty seconds. The colors morphed into even more dreadful hallucinations. Extra rasping heads sprouted from the hairy back of the monster, whispering Damien's name with inhuman vocal cords.

"It's your fault your mother is alone. She'll starve without you. You've killed her."

Thirty seconds. *No. Mother.*

One minute. *I just have to make it a week. Then I can go back.*

Black circles dotted his vision, expanding and blocking any illumination from the dull bioluminescent purple moss that peered through the soot on the brickwork as well as his hallucinations. He was dying. No one would mourn him.

The soot maven grew tired of inspecting the metal grating and lumbered on down the tunnel, leaving Damian to his blind terror.

Will those . . . silio petals . . . work in time? Did I not . . . take enough?

His own screams echoed in his mind. Coherent thoughts scattered.

What felt like metal bands constricting his chest began to lift as the last long leg of the soot maven rounded the far corner, out of view. Air flowed into Damian's lungs and his heart began to beat once again. He had survived one more hour.

Crack. A scream.

The sound was so out of place and unexpected that Damian undid the catch and lifted the grate to see where it had come from. No soot maven, dirt devil, varlet frog, or mud bug had ever made that noise before, only fellow soot scamps when being devoured. But there were none who ventured this far into the outskirts. Only the banished.

There, at the bend in the tunnel where the soot maven had come from, sat the most colorful creature Damian had ever seen. She looked like him, but different. Her face was not that of a soot scamp; she had human eyes that gleamed with wetness in the dark, reflecting the light she brought with her. She wore a dress with a full skirt of yellow. He had never seen so much of that color before. Above her was a split in the ceiling. Rubble lay around her. The light strapped to her head was brighter than all the plants he had ever seen and had the tint of many colors. Red, green, yellow, blue, and purple.

It took her a few minutes to get her bearings, peering into the surrounding darkness. Finally, her eyes alighted on him. With a gasp, she cried out. "Oh, thank heavens. Where—"

He sprang to her and clamped his grimy hand over her mouth. *Don't make a sound. You'll be hunted and eaten*, Damian signed with his free hand. *They're probably already on their way.*

Her wide eyes stared into his recessed ones as she nodded her understanding. He released her, and she took a step back, shaken.

Who are you? Damian signed.

The girl raised a trembling hand and signed, *Rebecca.*

What is that light? he inquired.

The lamp? Don't you have lamps on this level? She looked up at her layer of the labyrinth with longing. *How do you see without them? This moss gives off hardly anything to see by.*

We make do. You'll get used to it.

"Get—"

He silenced her yet again with his hand.

I'm not staying here long enough to get used to it. Give me a boost and I can climb back up. You can come with me! Her bright eyes glowed.

The proposition was tempting. He could escape the soot mavens. He wouldn't have to live alone in constant danger for the rest of the week.

Stories of the other levels flooded his mind. Here there were known dangers; up there was where myths lived. Yet, one was standing in front of him. A pure-blooded human. Not a half-breed like the soot scamps.

Skritch. Skritch.

Looking down the tunnel, Damian saw the soot maven had returned. A lumbering skuttle told him another soot maven was at the other end too. It was too late to hide, douse the light, and stop their hearts. They would have to climb to the next level if they wanted to live.

Damian slid back to the dry well and grabbed the prized grappling hook he used for navigating the collapsed and sunken parts of the labyrinth to scavenge for food. He threw it up into the rift above them and shoved the girl to the rope.

The soot mavens were now close enough that Rebecca could see them against the black coal-dusted walls. She screamed and started shimmying up the rope as fast as she could.

Claws swiped at Damian's shoes, slicing his soles as he followed her and her light into the bright unknown. The girl clambered up to the next level and reached her hand down for him. He took it and pulled himself up. They were safe.

The lantern was blinding to Damian, especially with the obsidian walls reflecting its rainbow colors. So strange. He ran his fingers down the hewn walls to examine their sharp, chipped smoothness. There was no new soot coating his rough hands when he pulled them back to inspect them.

"Thank you," Rebecca gasped, lying on the floor a few feet away from the opening. Her gasps were sharp and labored. Damian had been taught at a young age to never breathe that loudly. "What's your name?"

Damian. Where are we? he signed. He squinted through the steady light emanating from the lantern still strapped to Rebecca's head.

"Oh, you can talk up here. Nothing too big is attracted to noise." She chuckled.

Would she lie to him? It was too risky. *Never talk outside the citadel.* The lesson rang in his mind. He signed the question again.

"Well, we're on the outskirts of the labyrinth. Tunnel 594, Offshoot B, if you want to be precise." She got up, dusted off her dress, and adjusted the lantern.

Slowly his eyes adjusted to the incessant light and blinding colors. It was some kind of bright illumination contained in an array of scavenged chips of colored glass from broken bottles and other paraphernalia, splashing the walls with brilliant hues. Rebecca's face was cast in red while the rest of her was in blue and yellow, her skirt now mixing with the light into swaths of green.

Finally, he noticed a thin, taut cord leading from her lower back, trailing off into the comfortingly dark tunnels. *Where does that lead?* he signed.

"Oh, it's so I don't get lost. It leads back to the main citadel. I should probably go back. Come with me?" Her voice was soft and sweet. Inviting.

I'm an outcast.

"Not here, you're not. Besides, it's dangerous to be out here alone in the dark, and I don't know how long it will take those creatures down below to leave. You're here already. Might as well make the most of it before going back home." She looked at him with pleading eyes. "At least meet my family so I can thank you for saving my life."

Damian gave a silent sigh. *All right. But then we come back here tomorrow. The soot mavens should be gone by then.*

"Deal. Now follow me." She turned on her heel and began following the cord down the tunnel, her multifaceted lantern illuminating the way. The colors reflected in mesmerizing patterns off the irregularly chipped walls, disorienting Damian with their beauty. He stayed behind Rebecca a few feet as she led the way.

Left. Right. Middle. Far right. Second left. Right. Damian tried to keep tabs of the directions in his head so he could find his way back himself if necessary. After the twelfth turn, he gave it up as a bad job. He could hear mining pickaxes in the side tunnels they did not go down, so at least they weren't completely alone. He could find help if they got separated.

The air pressure was different in this section of the labyrinth, a rhythmic wind gently caressing his skin. A large cavern opened ahead of them. It was the largest Damian had ever seen. At the back of it was a large, towering city of stone with many lights twinkling in windows.

Wow. Do no dangerous creatures come to check out all the lights? he signed.

"Sometimes, but we know how to defend ourselves from them. It's worth it." She scrambled over well-worn rocks toward what looked like a gap in the rockwork that was the front entrance to the city of light.

The city seemed to breathe, yet there were no people visible from this distance. The silence of no words spoken aloud was comforting to him yet seemed off if Rebecca's behavior was anything to go by. He slowed down to take in more of his surroundings.

Water dripped from the vaulted ceiling high above, causing an incessant small splash every few seconds to his right. The air rushed into the cave, then out. In, out. Why would the current change so often in such opposite directions? His guts squirmed in trepidation.

"What are you doing, Damian?" Rebecca called out from farther ahead. Her dress billowed in the breeze; a beautiful sight. So much yellow.

He didn't trust her anymore.

He turned and began to run back toward the entrance of the cave.

"No!" The girl's voice morphed and deepened, vibrating off the rock walls.

The vibrations intensified, and the ground rumbled. Damian looked back and saw the city move, its towers swaying precariously, yet the lights never went out. Instead, they began to flash in patterns along the length of the city from front to back, like they did on mud bugs. Huge sections of the stonework separated from each other like shifting continents, revealing the pale squishy flesh of a creature. Tendrils shot out from its soft body like sharp spikes seeking him out.

Damian couldn't help it and screamed for the first time since his mother had slapped him to shut him up when he'd been five. Antennae-like appendages speared through his stomach, impaling him like a varlet frog on a stick. His screams became hoarse and wet. He was a dead man.

Desperately, he looked to Rebecca. She was limp and hanging high in the air, a glowing lure no longer animated that had brought him to his death. Her job was complete. She had never really been a human. He had fallen for it.

A deep animalistic chuckle echoed from the city-camouflaged creature. He was going to be eaten. There was nothing he could do about it.

Reaching deep into the pocket of his overalls, he pulled out a clump of black cortardo leaves and placed them in his mouth. No need for the silio petals. He would not live to feel the piercing teeth or burning stomach acid of the abomination.

His chest constricted tightly, his lungs burning for air, his vision darkening, comfortingly familiar.

His final whisper: "Mom, I'm sorry."

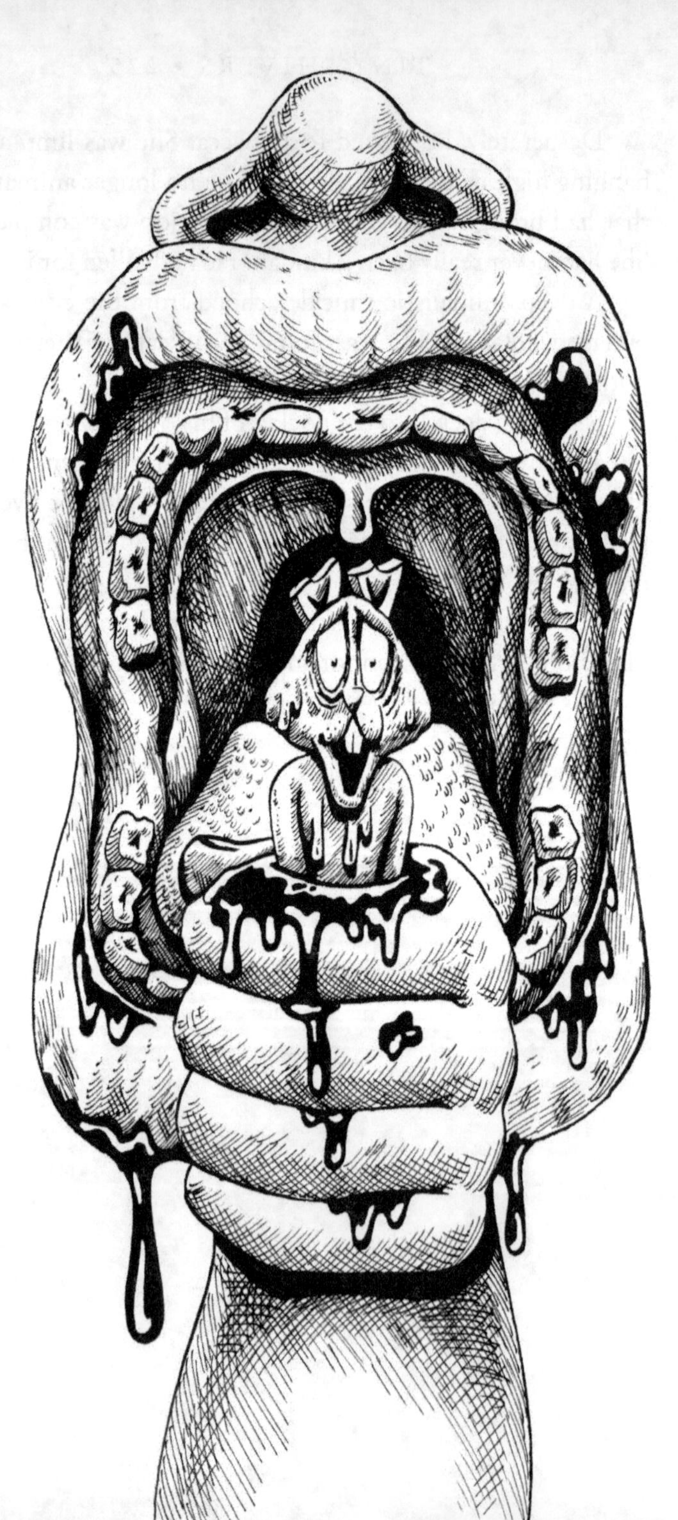

HOLIDAY FOOD HORROR

Easter Bunny

MR. EASTER BUNNY GLANCED AROUND the basket filled with fake grass and other candy he had been placed in. The mini eggs cowered among the shredded plastic, trying to burrow their way to freedom. The shrill laugh of a human child sent chills down his chocolate spine. He started sweating, a film of bloom creeping along his formerly pristine shell. More shrieks echoed in the hall. They were coming, the hell spawn his mother had warned him about.

Suddenly, he was lifted from his warm seat. His shiny foil was ripped from around him, leaving him naked and afraid in the hot hands of a demon.

Crunch.

His ears were the first thing to go.

Deviled Eggs

MY INSIDES WENT THROUGH THE blender, shredding and tearing my essence. Pulverized. Mixed with unholy additions—mayo, salt, paprika. The hollow of my body was refilled with my remade self.

I will never be the same.

Ms. Fruitcake

MS. FRUITCAKE KNEW WHAT IT felt like to be unloved. She'd been passed from person to person, and no one would sample from her lovingly baked wares. Raisins, figs, prunes, cherries, apricots, and peaches had all been soaked in rum before being gently folded into her embrace. And yet, no one would touch her. What had she done to offend them? The vapors of alcohol rising from her surface distorted her view of the humans looking down upon her. They wrinkled their noses in disdain at the sight of her.

"Who likes fruitcake?" a particularly loud woman asked.

After the party, Ms. Fruitcake sipped more rum, drowning her sorrows. Her baker, the lonely Mrs. Johnson, also imbibed. Together, they commiserated their losses.

At least they had each other.

Shortbread

HAROLD, THE REINDEER-SHAPED SHORTBREAD, looked at his brethren on their red paper plate. They had been saved from the children at home by the proactive

Saran Wrap shielding around them and slaps to the gremlin's hands from Mother. Now, though, they had arrived at a new destination. A welcome mat on a doorstep. The doorbell of doom rang out while the gremlins scattered, hiding behind a bush.

Harold held his breath in anticipation. What was coming?

A coffin-like creak resounded as the huge door opened. A furry creature bounded upon them, slobbering all over their shielding, but it held. Terror shivered through Harold's colored sugar sprinkles when he saw the claws. Nails each the size of Harold rained down upon them, slicing through their only defense.

The drooling jaws of death descended, sending them scattering across the porch. Antlers detached, red sugar dissolved in the strings of saliva.

Harold's glutenous heart became crumbs.

Marshmallow

THE MALLOW SCREAMED IN AGONY as his flesh softened and melted into the steaming hot cocoa he was currently drowning in. Monstrous eyes peered over the rim of the mug at his predicament. Methodically, they submerged him over and over with the cold metallic tip of a spoon.

His lungs filled with the chocolaty fluid, melting him from the inside as well. His sense of self disintegrated along with his body. Foam became his headstone.

Candy Canes

I WAS BORN IN THE fiery copper pot where my elements melted together. My first words were hisses of pain as I bubbled and boiled. Poured out onto unfeeling metal, I was bent in on myself over and over until I had been contorted a thousand times. My steaming voice was gone from overuse. As I rested, chunks of my body were torn away and dyed with festive color. Before I could recover, I was weightless as my body was lifted through the air and draped over a candy hook. My body oozed down with the weight of my own flesh. Then the candymaker pulled me. Over and over. I was stretched, roped, and aerated. Transmuted to the color of bone. White with my colored limbs returned, then stretched and twisted to the edge of my capacity. No voice escaped me now. I was cut into pieces and bent into hooks, my remains put on display.

Gingerbread

MR. GINGERBREAD STARED DOWN AT his broken-off leg. His bloodless body still felt shock. Quickly, before more crumbs disintegrated from the wound, he grabbed the piping bag of royal icing and went to work. No needle could pierce him without disastrous results. It had to be glue, of the edible variety. Edible to humans. Not gingerbread men. That would be weird.

The heavy bag sagged in his shaking, mitten-shaped hands. One after another, white stitch-like patterns were laid across his cookie flesh. Now to dry. He lay in stillness, listening to the cacophony of Christmas carols filling the room.

Thump. Thump. Thump.

No.

A human child reached for him, lifting his aching body from his rest. The icing was not yet dry. His leg dangled by an icicle and fell back to the base of the house made of flesh.

Crunch.

Mr. Gingerbread knew no more.

Laura is a California girl living in Toronto, Canada. She works in the film industry, lighting many monsters for both movies and television. She graduated from BYU's animation program in 2015 and has been working up in the snow ever since. She mostly writes adult and middle grade horror, but has some sci-fi and dark fantasy stories mulling around his her brain as well. When she's not writing, she is petting her dog Roy and drinking rooibos tea.

WWW.LAURANETTLES.COM